Novels by Ariel Tachna

Château d'Eternité
Fallout
Her Two Dads
Inherit the Sky • Chase the Stars • Outlast the Night
The Inventor's Companion
The Matelot
Once in a Lifetime
Overdrive
Out of the Fire
Seducing C.C.
Stolen Moments
A Summer Place

The Partnership in Blood Novels
Alliance in Blood • Covenant in Blood • Conflict in Blood • Reparation in Blood
Perilous Partnership
Reluctant Partnerships
Lycan Partnership

With Nicki Bennett
Checkmate • All For One
Hot Cargo
Under the Skin

With Madeleine Urban
Sutcliffe Cove

OUTLAST THE NIGHT

ARIEL TACHNA

Dreamspinner Press

Published by
Dreamspinner Press
5032 Capital Circle SW
Ste 2, PMB# 279
Tallahassee, FL 32305-7886
USA
http://www.dreamspinnerpress.com/

Outlast the Night
Copyright © 2013 by Ariel Tachna

Cover Art by Anne Cain
annecain.art@gmail.com

ISBN: 978-1-62380-708-5
Digital ISBN: 978-1-62380-709-2

Printed in the United States of America
First Edition
May 2013

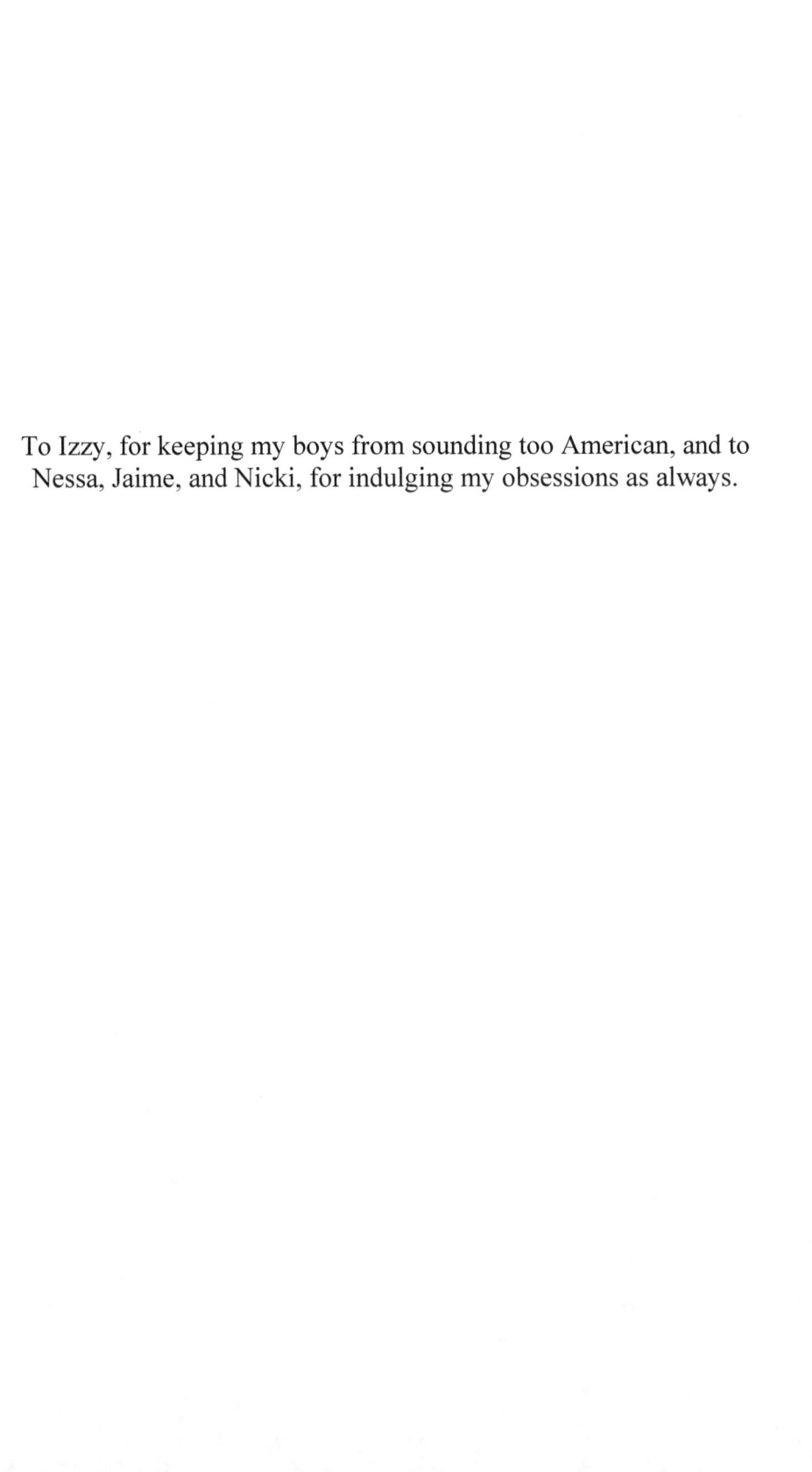

To Izzy, for keeping my boys from sounding too American, and to Nessa, Jaime, and Nicki, for indulging my obsessions as always.

ONE

CAINE NEIHEISEL looked up from the tax forms that were currently driving him batty when he heard a knock at the office door. It wouldn't be Macklin because his lover and the foreman of Lang Downs wouldn't bother knocking.

"Come in."

"I'm sorry to disturb you, boss," Neil Emery said, sticking his head in. "Do you have a minute?"

"Of course," Caine said, setting aside the forms. "What can I do for you?"

"I need a favor. My brother Sam called. His wife kicked him out, and he doesn't have anywhere else to go. He lost his job a year and a half ago, and I know it's a lot to ask, but could he come here for a month or two? Just until he gets back on his feet?"

"The last time I checked, you and Molly had an extra room in your house. You don't need my permission to have someone stay there."

"I'll have to go down to Yass to get him," Neil said. "I can send him a bus ticket to get that far, but it'll still mean taking at least a day off."

"Just let us know when you'll be gone so we can get someone to cover your chores."

"I'll leave Max with Chris. Chris has learned enough about dogs that he can use Max to help move the sheep down into the valley. I know it's a bad time to be gone, but I can't afford to pay for a hotel for him for long—"

"Neil," Caine interrupted, "I'm not upset. He's your brother. Of course you're going to help him out. I don't know how much luck he'll have doing a job search from here, but even if all he does is recover from leaving his wife before figuring out how to go back to town, he's still welcome. We can afford to feed one more."

"He could maybe help you out in the office while he's here," Neil suggested. "He worked as an office manager for a small hardware store until the owners retired and closed the shop. At least he'd feel like he was contributing something instead of taking handouts."

"We'll see when he gets here," Caine said, though the idea of having someone to help him figure out the logistics of Australian tax law and employee benefits regulations would be a huge help. Caine's degree in business gave him enough background to make sense of the jargon, but the difference in laws had tripped him up more than once.

THREE days later, Neil met his brother Sam at the bus station in Yass. The lines of stress and worry on his brother's face made him frown. "You look like shit."

"Good to see you too, arsehole," Sam replied, hugging Neil more tightly than necessary.

"Come on," Neil said, grabbing Sam's sole suitcase. "Let's get out of here. We've got a long drive ahead of us. Or do you want to eat something first?"

"How long?"

"Five hours or so," Neil said, "and most of that is through the tablelands, where there's nowhere to stop if you get hungry. I can shout you lunch, here or in Boorowa in an hour or so, if you don't think you can wait until we get home."

"Lunch would be good," Sam admitted. "I… haven't been eating well."

Neil had noticed how gaunt Sam looked, but this confirmed it. "Kami, the station's cook, will get you sorted in no time, but for now we can go to the Yass Hotel. It's nothing fancy, but it'll fill you up."

"What about that one?" Sam asked, pointing to a small restaurant across from the bus station.

"We don't eat there," Neil said, his voice cold. "One of our jackaroos nearly got killed there last spring, and nobody lifted a finger to help him. His brother had to come running to the hotel for help."

"In a town this size?"

"They didn't take well to him being a poofter," Neil explained.

Sam didn't reply. Neil gritted his teeth when he saw the tense look on Sam's face. He didn't want to fight with his brother, especially when he was down and out, but Sam was going to have to keep his opinions to himself. Neil wouldn't tolerate slurs against Caine and Macklin from his brother any more than he would from any of the other jackaroos on Lang Downs.

"So tell me about the station," Sam said once they'd reached the Yass Hotel and had ordered lunch. "I mean, I know it's kind of remote and I know you raise sheep, but that's as far as it goes."

"That's about all there is to tell," Neil said. "I told you about Molly when we got engaged. Everything else is pretty much what you'd expect from a station. Well, except Caine. He's a Yank. He owns the station."

"How did that happen?"

"His great-uncle founded the station. When he died, it passed to Caine's mum in the States, but she's not young and wasn't going to move here to run it, so Caine came. Last year at Christmas, she gave it to him outright. You know, I bet he could use a hand figuring out all the paperwork, taxes and shit. He's got a head for business, but he's still a Yank. You could keep your hand in."

"If he'll let me help," Sam said with a sigh.

"Why wouldn't he?" Neil asked. "You lost your job because the owners retired. You weren't fired or laid off or anything like that. It's not your fault you couldn't find a new job."

Sam shrugged. "He sounds like a good bloke. Is he married?"

Neil choked on his beer. He'd been hoping to put off this conversation until later, but short of lying, he didn't see a way around it. "Last time I checked, two blokes can't get married here. Macklin's name is on the deed, though, and he moved out of the foreman's house and into the big house a year ago, so I figure that's close enough."

"You work for a gay couple?"

"Sam, you're my brother and I love you, but if this is going to be a problem, you need to tell me now so I can get you a hotel room in Yass."

"No, it's not a problem," Sam said quickly. "I'm just surprised. We didn't exactly grow up in a tolerant house."

Neil shrugged. "Caine saved my life and nearly died doing it. And he did it after I found out he was gay and said every nasty thing I could think of to him. He's earned my loyalty."

The arrival of their food forestalled Sam's reply, and he ate with such gusto that Neil didn't press for more of a reaction. He wasn't in the mood to listen to all the homophobic bullshit he'd grown up with. He was a different man now, a better one, he hoped. If Sam could just give Caine and Macklin a chance, he'd see they deserved his respect.

They finished eating and headed north toward Boorowa. "Do you need anything?" Neil asked. "Supplies of any kind? Once we leave Boorowa, there's nowhere to stop."

"No, I'm fine," Sam said. "Alison let me keep everything of mine."

"One suitcase?" Neil responded.

"I left some stuff with friends," Sam said. "I didn't figure I'd need suits on the station."

"No, you won't," Neil agreed. "So tell me. What happened with you and Alison? Last time I saw you, I thought you were happy."

"She wanted someone with a job, and I wanted…. It doesn't matter what I wanted. She wanted out, and I'm not going to fight her."

"Is there someone else?" Neil asked.

"I didn't ask her," Sam said.

"What about you?"

"No one that matters."

"You slept around and it didn't even mean anything? That's low, Sam."

"It wasn't like that," Sam insisted. "I...."

"You what, Sam?"

"I married her because it's what Mum and Dad expected. I didn't feel like I had a choice, and at least I liked Alison. We got along well enough, but that's it. I never really loved her. I don't know if she loved me, but she doesn't anymore, and I'm fine with that. Dad's gone. He can't be disappointed in me now, so it doesn't matter anymore."

"What are you talking about? Why would you marry Alison if you didn't love her? You could have found someone else."

"You already said it," Sam said. "It's not legal for two blokes to get married."

"You're gay? Why didn't you say something?" The words were out before Neil could consider them, the only thing he could think of to say in the wake of such surprising news. Sam had been married! Neil had never dreamed his brother might be gay.

Sam shot him a look of such incredulity that Neil flushed. "Sorry, that was stupid. Of course you didn't say anything while Dad was alive, but you still didn't have to get married. I didn't. Not until I met the right girl."

"Yeah, but you aren't gay. You might not have met the right girl, but you knew you would someday. I didn't have that, and you were gone. You didn't have to listen to him constantly after you left, going on and on about the family name and being a man and getting married and having children. Thank God Alison and I decided to wait to have kids."

"Did she know about you?"

"Not when we got married. After I lost my job and couldn't find another one, things got... tense at home. Money was tight. I felt like a failure for living off her income. We fought all the time. We agreed to a trial separation nine months ago, with her helping me out with the rent, but I think that was almost worse, because she was supporting me completely. I wanted to feel good. I wanted to spend a few hours with someone who didn't make me feel worthless."

"So you did what? Hooked up with some random guys?"

"Yeah, pretty much," Sam said. "It was stupid. I knew it when I did it, but it felt good too. They didn't care that I didn't have a job. They didn't care that I was in the closet. They just cared that I'd let them do whatever they wanted to me. Alison kept on about getting a new job, always threatening to stop paying my rent if I didn't get my act together. She actually had a lead on one, but it was with a cousin of hers, and he made it pretty obvious he'd only be hiring me out of pity. I turned down the job and told her I'd find somewhere else to live. There's no way I could go back to that."

"I wish I'd known," Neil said. "I'd have tried to make it easier for you."

"There's nothing you could have done," Sam said. "I had to fuck up to see how bad off I was."

"So what now?"

"Now nothing," Sam said. "I won't fight Alison for anything when we can finally file for divorce in three months. She gets the house, the car, everything, because she's paid for most of it, and I don't want the black mark on my name if I ever get a lead on a job somewhere that might care if I'm gay."

"There's not a lot of opportunity for anonymous sex, gay or straight, on the station," Neil warned. "There's a couple of other jackaroos who are gay besides Caine and Macklin, but Chris and Jesse are shacked up, and the others will be leaving when the season is over in a few weeks."

"So I'll do without," Sam said with a shrug. "It won't be the first time." He hesitated, then added, "I got enough of faceless fumbling this year. I'd rather do without until I can meet someone. I know that probably won't happen on the station, and really, starting a relationship before I'm even divorced would be stupid, but I'd rather do without than feel like a cheap trick again."

"I thought you said it made you feel good?"

"The sex, yes. Afterward, no," Sam explained. "I don't imagine you want details."

"Not really," Neil said with a grimace. "I might not let anyone say anything about Caine and Macklin, but I don't need to know what goes on in their bedroom. Same goes for you."

Sam's smile was the most genuine Neil had seen since he'd picked his brother up at the bus station.

"Thank you."

"YOU need to go to Melbourne this winter," Devlin Taylor said, turning to face his younger brother Jeremy. "You need to find a good woman, settle down, start a family."

Jeremy only barely managed not to roll his eyes at his brother across the breakfast table in the main house. Devlin refused to eat in the canteen with the jackaroos. He said it was "beneath him." They had been through this discussion of his relationship status more times than he could count. He would get married when he was damn well ready—not likely to happen anytime soon since he wasn't going to marry a woman and he couldn't legally marry a man—and Devlin could take his meddling and matchmaking and shove them up his arse. "I was planning a trip to Sydney," Jeremy replied, "but just for a week or two, to unwind a bit from the summer."

"That's not long enough to meet someone," Devlin protested.

"Maybe because I don't *want* to meet someone?" Jeremy retorted. "Not like that. We aren't having this conversation again."

"Be careful, boy," Devlin said as if he were Jeremy's father, not his older brother. Granted, the twelve years between them meant he and Devlin had never been all that close, never had the shared childhood so many siblings drew on to bond as adults. "People will start talking. You're thirty-four. That's more than old enough to get settled down proper. You keep on like you are, people are going to start saying you're like those pillow biters up at Lang Downs."

"So what if they think that?" Jeremy replied hotly, not the least because it was true. He hated the term as much as he hated his brother's homophobic rants, but he could hardly deny he was gay, even if he had conveniently forgotten to tell his brother that one important detail. "Armstrong runs a tight ship at Lang Downs, regardless of who he's sleeping with, and when you had to fire that fucker who sabotaged their fences, Neiheisel let it go without pursuing you or him. They aren't hurting anybody by being together."

"No brother of mine is going to be known as a poofter!" Devlin roared.

"Better an honest poofter than a homophobic bigot who still can't run a station as well as the 'pillow biters' at Lang Downs," Jeremy shouted back.

Devlin's angry bellow gave Jeremy the warning he needed to dodge the punch his brother sent flying in his direction. His own ire raised now, he countered with an uppercut of his own, catching his brother squarely under the jaw. Devlin staggered back, then narrowed his eyes as he came at Jeremy again. Jeremy tried to block the blow, but Devlin connected anyway. Jeremy rocked back, catching himself on the edge of the desk in Devlin's office, and slammed his brother's face into the wooden surface when Devlin lunged at him again. He had the briefest moment of relief that at least none of the jackaroos still on the station would see them fighting like this before Devlin was up again and plowing his fist into Jeremy's gut. He doubled over and went for Devlin's knees. When his brother went down, he stayed there, glaring at Jeremy with such hatred that Jeremy took a step back.

"Get out," Devlin spat, blood running from the corner of his mouth. "Don't come back until you've got a wife and a respectable life."

Jeremy closed his eyes for a second, knowing from the tone of Devlin's voice how deadly serious he was. "I'll be gone before sunset."

"And don't take anything that belongs to the station," Devlin added.

That would be impossible, since Jeremy had never bothered drawing a salary and bought what he needed with station funds the same way Devlin did, but Jeremy was tired of arguing with his brother. He would take what he considered to be his personal belongings and leave the rest. He could replace anything else once he got a job on another station. He hoped Lang Downs was hiring because that would be an extra punch to his brother's gut, but if they weren't, Jeremy figured he had enough experience to get a job pretty much anywhere.

He climbed the stairs to his room, rubbing his jaw where Devlin's fist had caught him, and proceeded to pack his clothes and toiletries. He considered taking his phone but decided Devlin would just cancel the contract if he did since it was on the station's account. Looking at the duffel that contained everything in the world he could truly consider his, he scowled at the sorry state of his life. He should have done this years ago.

"I'm taking my car," he told Devlin when he got downstairs. "I'll send it back when I get where I'm going."

Devlin didn't even look up from where he sat at his desk, a cold pack on his lip.

Jeremy turned on his heel and walked out of the house where he'd grown up, whistling for Arrow, his kelpie, as he went. It was time to shake the dust of Taylor Peak off his feet.

"IT'S too early for Neil to be back, isn't it?" Caine asked Macklin, looking down the valley at the plume of dust from the gravel road.

"I wasn't expecting him before dinner," Macklin said, following Caine's gaze.

"Are we expecting anyone else?"

"Not that I was aware of," Macklin said. "I guess we should go see who it is."

"I can handle it if you want to stay here and finish getting the sheep settled," Caine offered, though he knew Macklin would refuse.

"No, I'll go with you," Macklin said.

Caine gave his lover an indulgent smile. He still hadn't figured out what kind of trouble Macklin thought he would get into walking across the valley by himself, especially since Polly, Jason's dog, had been on Caine's heels all day and didn't seem inclined to leave now, but Caine didn't argue either. He *could* handle whatever or whoever was driving down their road by himself, but that didn't mean he would enjoy it, depending on what it was.

As the dust cloud approached, Caine could make out a plain black Jeep much like the ones they used at Lang Downs for trips to town. Eventually it pulled up to where they were standing and a man Caine didn't know climbed out, followed by a solid brown kelpie with the bluest eyes Caine had ever seen on a dog.

"Taylor?" Macklin said, tensing at Caine's side. "What are you doing here?"

Taylor meant Taylor Peak, and that meant their jackass of a neighbor, but this wasn't Devlin Taylor. This man was closer to Caine's age than Macklin's, and much more the typical jackaroo than Devlin Taylor could ever hope to be.

"Sorry to arrive uninvited," Taylor said, "but my brother kicked me off the station. I'm hoping you've got space for one more, for a day or two, anyway."

"Why did he kick you out?" Macklin asked.

"I got tired of listening to his bullshit," Taylor said. "I called him on it and he didn't take it well."

"That how you got the shiner?" Macklin asked.

"Yeah, but it was worth it," Taylor replied. "The look on his face was priceless."

"What did you say?" Macklin asked, his voice sounding amused now.

"He was going on about you two, the way he does when he gets in a snit," Taylor said. "I told him I'd rather work for you than for a homophobic bigot who still couldn't run his station as well as the two men he was so determined to insult."

Caine couldn't stop the grin that crossed his face. "Caine Neiheisel," he said, holding out his hand to their guest. "Welcome to Lang Downs."

"Jeremy Taylor. Nice to finally meet you."

"So are you looking for a place to crash for a few days or are you looking for a job?" Macklin asked after Caine and Jeremy had shaken hands.

"A job, if you've got one, but at this point, I'll settle for not having to drive to Boorowa tonight."

"The foreman's position is already taken," Macklin said, not quite cracking a smile, although Caine thought he heard amusement in the words, "but we've got space in the bunkhouse."

"It's a roof over my head," Taylor said. "That's good enough for me."

"Come on, then. We'll find you a bunk," Macklin said. "Caine, you want to tell Kami there will be one more for dinner?"

"Of course," Caine said, even though he was dying to go with them and find out more about their newest stray. But he would have time. He didn't have to know everything right now.

"So you want to tell me what was different this time?" Macklin asked as he led Jeremy toward the bunkhouse, Arrow following on their heels. "Devlin's been shouting filth in our direction for more than a year, since he found out about Caine, and he's been pressuring you to fit into his mold for longer than that."

"He started in about me getting married," Jeremy said. "Same shit, different day, but today I just got tired of it. He can shout and threaten all he wants. I'm not getting married because of it, and I got sick of listening to it."

"That station is your birthright too."

Jeremy shook his head. "Not in any way that counts. His name's on the deed. Maybe Dad meant for us to run it together, but he didn't give me any actual say in it in any kind of legal way that I could enforce. I was at uni still when he died, so maybe that made a difference. Who knows? I've spent more than ten years being ignored every time I've tried to point out to Devlin a way to improve something. Never mind that I'm the one with the degree in animal management, not him. I'm his kid brother, so I don't know anything. I got tired of it, and listening to him insult you was one thing too many."

"You know the rumors that are going to make the rounds since you came here instead of going to a different station," Macklin said. "Nobody here cares what the gossips have to say, but it might make going somewhere else later harder than if you went to a different station."

Jeremy shrugged. "They won't be saying anything that isn't true. Maybe I never told anybody. Maybe I'd never planned on telling anybody, but that doesn't make it less true."

Macklin just nodded like he'd known all along, making Jeremy wonder what was going on behind that inscrutable stockman mask Jeremy knew so well. He'd put it on himself so many mornings he wasn't sure how to take it off anymore. Had Macklin suspected? Or did he simply accept it that easily? Jeremy wasn't sure it mattered, and it made him more grateful than he could say.

"It's up to you what you tell people or don't," Macklin said as they reached the bunkhouse. "I'm not one for telling tales."

"Thanks," Jeremy said. "It'll be hard enough in there, being a Taylor. Being gay won't help."

"Depends on who you're talking to," Macklin said with a grin. "Some of them might consider that a point in your favor."

"I'm here to work, not to fuck around," Jeremy said. "I'm not interested in a relationship."

Macklin laughed. "Where have I heard that before? I appreciate the attitude, but as long as the work's done, the rest is up to you and whoever you choose to spend your time with. I don't keep tabs on my men's personal lives unless they interfere with the job."

They went inside and peeked in rooms until they found an empty bunk. "You can take a few minutes to unpack if you want," Macklin offered. "You can meet us at the sheds."

"And have someone come in and see me and think I'm here without your permission?" Jeremy said, tossing his duffel on the bed. "I'll unpack tonight after work. By then hopefully everyone will realize I'm here with your blessing."

"Most of the ones here in the bunkhouse are too new to remember the dustup with Devlin," Macklin replied. "They might recognize your name, but it's only the year-rounders, who tend to have houses of their own, who might have an issue with you."

Jeremy wasn't sure if that made things better or worse. The jackaroos in the bunkhouse would be leaving in a few weeks, for the most part, off to wherever they spent the winter once the bulk of the work from breeding was done. Jeremy would have the bunkhouse pretty much to himself after that, but the men he would have to work with when the seasonal hires were gone all knew his family, his brother, and the ongoing animosity between the two stations. Or, to be fair, the ongoing animosity Devlin felt toward Lang Downs. Jeremy had never shared that sentiment, even before Caine's arrival and finding out both he and Macklin were gay, but while Macklin knew that, Jeremy doubted the others would.

"I'll still make a better impression by coming to work now, since I know there's work to be done," Jeremy said.

"There's always work to be done," Macklin said with a shrug.

"Then let's get to it," Jeremy said. "Come on, Arrow."

TWO

NEIL pulled his car behind the house he identified to Sam as his and Molly's. "We'll put your bag inside. You can unpack later. It's dinnertime, and you don't want to miss whatever Kami has cooked up for us."

Sam set his bag inside the door and followed Neil across the station. He'd worn his sturdiest shoes, but now he wished he had taken Neil up on his offer to buy him some boots in Boorowa. His shoes would be ruined in a matter of days. He'd already asked Neil for so much, though. He couldn't ask for more. The canteen was full of men in line to get food from the huge aborigine on the other side of the counter, some men already at tables, eating, and a few who looked like they'd already finished. He didn't let his eyes linger as he took in the scene. He wasn't known here, and while Neil had said people accepted the bosses, Sam was an unknown quantity. He didn't want to start his first evening with a fight. If Neil was right and Caine might hire Sam for his experience as an office manager, fighting or causing a fight was not the right first impression to make.

Despite himself, though, his gaze lingered on a man sitting off at a table by himself. Sam couldn't have said what set that man apart from a room full of stockmen, besides being the only man sitting alone, but the dirty-blond hair, slightly spiky, like he'd run his hands through it more than once, and the shadow of a day's growth on his chin and cheeks called to something in Sam. The man radiated masculinity, and Sam couldn't help reacting. "Who's that?" he asked Neil, trying not to stare too obviously.

"Bloody hell," Neil spat. "What is he doing here?"

Before Sam could ask what that meant, Neil was striding across the room. The man who had caught Sam's eye saw him coming and stood, hands at his side but clearly braced for a fight. A third man, one who looked as hard as the granite beneath their feet, interrupted Neil's progress. "Don't blame one man for his brother's faults."

"What's he doing here?" Neil repeated.

Deeming it safe, Sam drew closer, wanting to learn what he could about the man and Neil's reaction to him.

"Working," the older man said. "Caine hired him this morning, so unless you want to argue with him over it, back off."

Sam tensed, knowing how badly Neil reacted to those kinds of orders when his temper was high. His jaw dropped when Neil shook himself and took a step back. "If Caine hired him, I won't make trouble, but if he starts anything, I will finish it."

"That's fair, Macklin," the other man said from his place against the wall. "You know I'm not going to start anything, so as long as he keeps his word, we'll be square."

"I keep my word, Taylor," Neil ground out. "Unlike some people."

"Neil, that's enough." Another man entered the conversation, a younger one, with short dark hair and an American accent. Sam figured that must be Caine. "Jeremy asked for a place to stay and a job after he left Taylor Peak. I've given him that. I'd appreciate it if you respect that."

Neil visibly deflated. "Yes, boss. I'm sorry."

"Introduce me to your brother."

Neil turned toward Sam. "Caine, this is my brother, Sam. Sam, my boss, Caine Neiheisel."

"Nice to meet you, sir," Sam said, even though Caine was probably Sam's age, maybe even a little less. He owed the man the roof over his head and maybe a job, if Neil was right. Sam planned to mind his manners.

"Please, call me Caine. We aren't formal here. Welcome to Lang Downs."

"Thank you. I appreciate you letting me stay for a while."

Caine smiled, and Sam felt warmth bloom inside at the kindness he saw there. It wasn't sexual. Sam knew Caine was with Macklin, and if Macklin was indeed the man who had kept Neil from attacking Taylor, Caine wouldn't look twice at someone like Sam. It felt almost familial, like he'd been adopted and hadn't known it until now. "Get something to eat—I know how hard the drive is from Yass—and get settled in tonight. Tomorrow I'd like to talk to you. I have some business questions, and Neil thought you might be able to help."

"I'm happy to help any way I can," Sam said. "I don't know a lot about sheep, but other than industry-specific regulations, the laws don't vary that much from one business to another. I should be able to help you out. And if I can't, I might know someone who can get the information we need."

"Good to hear," Caine said. "We'll talk about it after breakfast tomorrow. Did Neil warn you what time the day starts around here?"

"No," Sam said.

"Early," Neil replied. "Breakfast is at five unless there's a reason for it to be earlier. You don't have to come down then, but if you don't, you'll only get cold cereal until lunch. Kami has no patience with people who don't get their lazy arses out of bed."

"I'll be up," Sam said. "I don't want anyone to have to go out of their way for me."

"I'm going to finish my dinner," Caine said. "I'll look for you both in the morning."

Sam turned back to Neil as Caine walked back to where he had been sitting before Neil exploded. Sam would ask again later about Taylor and the reasons behind Neil's animosity. For now, the food smelled delicious, and Sam was getting hungry.

"What's for dinner?" he asked, smiling at the aborigine behind the counter when he approached.

"Wombat curry," the man—Kami, Sam thought Neil had said—replied.

"I've never had wombat before," Sam said, holding his plate while Kami ladled a thick stew onto his plate.

"You aren't having it now either," Neil said. "It's either beef or mutton, probably mutton. We are on a sheep station, after all. Kami likes to take the piss with blow-ins."

"And I fell for it."

"You're not the first, and you won't be the last," Kami said. "You want some naan with the curry?"

"Kami makes it fresh," Neil said. "It's as good or better than anything you ever got in town."

"Sure, I'll have a piece," Sam said. It wouldn't hurt to get on Kami's good side. The man would be feeding him for the foreseeable future. Better that Kami like him.

They found a seat at a table with several other men and a pretty woman who smacked Neil on the back of the head as soon as he sat down. "What was that?" she demanded.

"Not here, Molly, please," Neil said.

Sam hid his snicker behind a bite of curry. He had never imagined Neil looking quite so henpecked. "Fine," Molly said, not sounding at all pacified, "but we will discuss this when we get home."

Neil looked so mortified that Sam took pity on him. "Hi," he said, "I'm Sam, Neil's brother."

Molly looked like she wanted to smack Neil again. "No manners," she muttered with an affectionate glare in her fiancé's direction. "Nice to meet you, Sam. I'm Molly. Welcome to Lang Downs."

"Thank you. Everyone has been very kind."

"It's that kind of place," Molly said, "which is why we're going to discuss Neil's outburst later. He's second in line behind Macklin. He can't go around acting stupid, or he's going to lose his place."

"It's Jeremy Taylor," Neil said with a frown. "What was I supposed to think?"

"That your bosses pay enough attention to who's in their canteen to realize he was there and that if they know he's there and don't have a problem with it, you shouldn't either?" Molly suggested.

"Taylor?" Sam repeated. "Like the neighboring station?"

"Yes, that Taylor," Neil said. "Well, the younger brother, but that family. I said I wouldn't start anything, and I won't, but I don't trust him. Devlin Taylor wouldn't know good management if it bit him in the arse."

Sam glanced at Taylor across the room, wondering what had led the other man to leave his home and come here instead. Taylor rose as Sam was looking that way, dumped his plate in the bin of dirty dishes, and headed outside. Sam couldn't help but think the man looked lonely.

"IT'S not fancy," Neil said, opening the door to the guest room in the foreman's house. "Molly's been fixing up our room, but she hasn't got to the other rooms yet. The plan was to work on the living room over the winter, but maybe she can do this one instead."

The room was plain, as Neil had said, but it was clean, and the linens on the bed smelled like summer rain. Sam didn't know how Molly had managed that on a dusty station in late autumn, but he wasn't about to complain. He ran his fingers over the embroidered bedspread. "Is this Mum's?"

"Yes," Neil said. "She sent some things when I told her Molly and I were setting up house."

"I thought I recognized it."

"Are you going to be okay in here by yourself?"

"I'm an adult," Sam said with affectionate exasperation, an emotion that seemed to be going around with regard to Neil tonight. "I think I can sleep in my own bed."

"You're sure you don't need anything?"

"Neil," Sam said, shooing his brother out the door, "go spend some time with your beautiful fiancée. I'll be fine. We have to get up for breakfast at five, and I'm not used to that schedule. I'm going to take a quick shower and then go to sleep. We'll figure everything else out in the morning."

Neil finally left, and Sam slumped down onto the bed. He needed a shower after the trip, but first he needed a few minutes alone. He had gotten used to living alone in his apartment. As wonderful as it was to see his brother, as freeing as it was to no longer be in the closet, Sam hadn't had a moment to himself since he left for Yass that morning.

He tried to take stock of his feelings the way the marriage counselor he and Alison had gone to for a few sessions had taught him. If he could identify what he was feeling and why, he could cope, the marriage counselor had insisted. Sam supposed the woman had been right in one sense. In identifying his dissatisfaction with living a lie, he had ended up out of that situation. Ended up depending on his brother's generosity.

It could be worse, Sam reminded himself. He could be living on the streets because Neil kicked him out after Sam told him he was gay.

It would take longer than a few hours to wrap his head around that surprise. He had devised a lot of ways to avoid the conversation, invented a lot of explanations if Neil demanded answers Sam didn't want to give. He had never dreamed of simply coming out to his brother. He'd planned to blame the situation on his job loss and Alison's impatience with his inability to find a new one. Then Neil had told Sam about his employers, had defended them against what he perceived as Sam's attitude toward them, and Sam had rolled the dice. He hadn't been that honest about his feelings with anyone since he realized he was attracted to the other boys in his class instead of the girls. Sam thought he could get used to the freedom to be himself. Caine wanted to talk business with him in the morning. Maybe that would lead to a temporary job.

He couldn't do anything about that tonight, though. He didn't have a computer to look up regulations concerning sheep stations or even to review tax laws. He'd have to hope his memory was good or that Caine had a computer he could use to check things if he had questions.

Muttering to himself about the pitfalls of self-pity, he stood to unpack his suitcase, hung up his couple of pairs of jeans, and folded his shirts into the drawers. When everything was unpacked, he grabbed his toiletries kit and headed down the hall to shower before bed.

JEREMY took off his boots at the door to the bunkhouse. He didn't know if the others would do the same, but his mum had raised him right. He never wore shoes inside anyone's living space. He spent too much time in dusty fields or in pens full of sheep dung to want to traipse that into the house. He smiled as Arrow appeared from somewhere to join him as he went inside.

"Did you have fun?" Jeremy asked, bending to scratch behind Arrow's soft ears. "You'd better be careful with Max. He's used to being top dog around here. I don't want you getting in any fights, okay?"

Arrow just stared at him in reply, tilting his head into the scratching fingers. Jeremy shook his head at his own foolishness. It wasn't like Arrow could actually understand him. "Do you think we'll be okay here? Macklin's giving us a chance, but that doesn't mean anyone else will."

He sighed, thinking about the confrontation, or near-confrontation, with Emery. The man had a reputation as a hothead, and Devlin certainly had given the men at Lang Downs plenty of reasons to distrust everyone at Taylor Peak, so the attitude wasn't unexpected. That didn't make it pleasant, though. If life at Lang Downs was going to be one conflict after another with Emery or, since Macklin had stopped the actual confrontation, constant sneers and comments, Jeremy wasn't sure he'd be able to stay. It would be harder to be open about being gay elsewhere, but he didn't want to live in a battle zone either, especially if he was forced into being one of the combatants.

He could hear laughter from the common area of the bunkhouse, the jackaroos unwinding after a long day. He imagined a few of them had cracked beers open. A few others had probably lit cigarettes. He thought he might even smell a hint of weed. He filed that away for further investigation. He wasn't about to start something on someone else's station the night he arrived, but he'd seen what happened up in Cowra when a jackaroo was busted for growing pot on the station he was working at. The station owner had very nearly gone down with him, and Jeremy didn't want that to happen to Caine and Macklin. He wouldn't even wish it on his brother, but he certainly wouldn't want to see it happen to his benefactors. If he smelled it again or saw any sign of it, he'd say something to Macklin in private.

He'd been toying with the idea of joining the others in the bunkhouse, hoping they didn't all share Emery's prejudices, but now he was hesitant to do so. He grabbed his toiletries and headed for the shower block instead. He'd get clean, get some rest, and deal with everything else tomorrow.

THREE

SAM could barely keep his eyes open at breakfast in the morning as he sucked down his cup of coffee. He needed the caffeine jolt to help him wake up if he was going to impress Caine with his business acumen after breakfast. Most of the jackaroos looked as bleary as Sam felt, but they were all heading out to work in the paddocks and fields, doing whatever it was needed doing in late autumn on a sheep station. They would have that physical activity to keep them awake. Sam would have only the caffeine and the sheer determination not to lose the one opportunity that had come his way since the Smiths closed their store eighteen months ago.

"Relax," Neil said, sitting down next to him. "Caine doesn't bite. He's the fairest man you'll ever meet."

"This is still a job interview," Sam replied, "no matter what terms you put it in. I'm a little out of practice."

"Maybe it is," Neil agreed, "but I'll repeat what I said: Caine is the fairest man you'll ever meet. If you can do what he needs you to do, that's all he'll require. I expected the worst when I heard a Yank was coming to run the station, but he was never afraid to get his hands dirty or ask questions if he didn't know something. He's never asked a man to do something he wasn't willing to do himself, which is why I'm still alive. He's not out to trip you up today. He just wants to know if you can help him."

Sam certainly hoped he could, but it wasn't that simple. He didn't know enough about what was involved in running a sheep station to know if he could help.

"If I can't, I guess I could always learn about sheep."

"That's the spirit," Neil said. "We taught Caine. I can teach you if it comes to that, but you'll be happier in the office, and Caine will be happier too."

"I can't believe how much you've mellowed," Sam said. "I never thought I'd see the day when you were so loyal to a gay man."

"It's not about that," Neil said. "They should have fired me for the way I acted after I found out about Caine, but they didn't, and then Caine saved my life. I'm loyal to two of the best men I know. The fact that they're a couple? Honestly, I try not to think about it, but it's nothing compared to what they've done for me."

"So if I meet someone one day?"

"You'll always be my brother," Neil replied. "And if you meet someone special and he makes you happy, that's what matters. I still won't want details, but I'm not Dad. Not anymore."

Sam smiled. "Any advice for my interview?"

"Don't bullshit him. If you don't know something, say so. You can look up and learn what you need to. He respects honesty more than anything else."

"Thanks," Sam said. "I'll remember that."

Sam finished eating, doing his best not to telegraph his unease to the rest of the room. Caine and Macklin sat at a nearby table talking with several other jackaroos Sam hadn't met yet, but it was obvious from the body language that they were well known to Caine and Macklin. Sam figured the two men knew everyone pretty well by the end of the summer, but it took a certain degree of familiarity to choose to sit at the table with the bosses. Two teens joined them at the table a moment later, obviously sure of their welcome, and Sam realized one of the boys closely resembled the youngest of the jackaroos.

"Chris and Seth Simms," Neil said, following Sam's gaze. "Chris is the one I was telling you about in Yass, the one who nearly died. Seth is his younger brother. And that's Jesse Harris sitting next to Chris, and then Jason Thompson, the other kid, and his dad, Patrick, our head mechanic. They're all year-rounders. Patrick's wife, Carley, is around here somewhere, although I haven't seen her this morning. She helps out in the bunkhouses and in the kitchen sometimes, when Kami lets her."

"You realize you're going to have to tell me all of this again in an hour," Sam said. "I've never been good at names."

"You'll have time to meet everyone," Neil said.

Caine and Macklin rose from their seats, then Macklin headed toward the door, and Caine came toward them. Neil tossed back the last of his coffee. "That's my signal to get to work. Good luck with your interview."

"Thanks. I'll see you at dinner."

Neil nodded and followed Macklin out the door.

"Don't rush," Caine said when Sam started to get up. "You can finish your breakfast. Just because Macklin believes the day can't start early enough doesn't mean we have to rush. You and I aren't trying to breed a thousand sheep in the next week."

"No, just figure out how to pay the men you employ and document it so everything adds up at the end of the year," Sam said.

"Yeah," Caine said. "Just that. I have a degree in business. That was supposed to be useful."

"I'm sure it is," Sam said, "but you got it at an American uni. If you were running the station over there, you'd know exactly what to do. I'll bet we can get it sorted in a few days. I had to do payroll and taxes for the Smiths when I ran the office at their shop. The scale is different here, but one employee or fifty or five hundred, you still have to pay them, deduct payroll taxes, and track benefits."

"Yes, and then there's deductions for supplies and all the rest," Caine said. "I know what would be deductible as a business expense back in the US, but not everything is the same. Every time I think I've got it figured out, I read something else and decide I don't understand it at all."

Sam finished the last of his eggs and picked up his coffee cup. The conversation had bolstered his courage. This might be a job interview, but Neil was right. Caine wasn't looking to trip him up. "Let's take a look, shall we?"

"Just let me refill my coffee."

Caine poured himself another cup of coffee and then led Sam into his office in the station house. For all that the building itself spoke of the age of the station, the interior of Caine's office was every bit as modern as anything Sam had seen in Melbourne.

"Nice place you got here," Sam commented.

Caine shrugged. "Uncle Michael still did everything in ledgers, although Macklin made him start using a computer the last few years, when his handwriting got illegible. I wasn't even going to try using his ledgers, and his computer was so out of date that it was almost as bad. I figured if I was going to spend the money to update the office, I might as well update it completely and then I wouldn't have to do it again anytime soon."

"Makes sense to me," Sam said. "It'll make my life easier too, so I'm not about to complain. Want to show me what you've got?"

Caine turned on the computer and angled the monitor so Sam could see as well. He pulled up the payroll records. "See, here's the problem," he said. "We pay them on a monthly basis, but we only employ them eight months of the year, so I'm pretty sure we're taking out too much in taxes, but I can't figure out the formula for the right amount."

Sam smiled. He could do this.

"JEREMY, Neil's gone with a couple others to bring a mob in from the north paddock, but there's another mob to the south. I've got bodies but no one with experience except Jesse, and he doesn't have a dog of his own," Macklin said.

"And bad weather is heading this way," Jeremy said, looking toward the highlands."

"Exactly. Will you go with Jesse? Technically he's in charge, but mostly because he knows where the sheep are."

"Yeah," Jeremy said. "I'll be his backup."

Jeremy whistled for Arrow and crossed the station to the paddock behind the breeding sheds where they kept the station's horses. A group of men had gathered, including the one Jeremy was looking for. "Harris?"

"Yeah, you riding with us today?"

"Macklin asked me to, yes," Jeremy said neutrally.

"Well, saddle up. Daylight's wasting."

Jeremy hid the relief he felt at Harris's words. He'd met with such hostility from so many quarters since his arrival that he'd started to expect the worst. Harris, at least, didn't seem bothered by his presence.

"I don't know the station's stock. Got a suggestion which one I should ride?"

"Any of them except Ned," Harris said, indicating a big sorrel gelding. "That one's Macklin's, and I've never seen anyone else even stay on him."

From Emery, that would have been thrown out as a challenge, but Harris apparently intended it as a simple statement of fact.

"Then I'd better pick a different one," Jeremy said with a grin. "I shouldn't start my first full day on the station getting thrown like the greenest blow-in."

Harris grinned back.

Jeremy threw the tack on the closest horse, a big bay mare, and mounted up. "Lead the way, boss," he called to Harris. "Daylight's wasting."

Harris laughed and headed toward the far end of the valley. Once they were outside the valley gate, he led them off the roads and up onto the tablelands, heading steadily south. Jeremy studied the men around him. The youngest of the bunch, Simms, Jeremy thought his name was, rode closest to Harris, clearly at ease with the other man if not so at ease with his horse. He didn't make obvious mistakes, but the way he sat in the saddle showed a lack of experience. The others were almost as ill at ease with their horses and didn't seem much more comfortable with Harris. It made Jeremy wonder just what had gone on that summer at Lang Downs.

Despite the apparent inexperience of the jackaroos riding with them, the station didn't show any signs of neglect, which was good, but it still made Jeremy curious. The last time he had visited Lang Downs—three years ago, at least—everything had seemed to run almost by itself, as if everyone knew what needed to be done without being told. He doubted most of the men he was riding with today had the slightest idea what they were doing beyond following orders. He wanted to ask but wasn't sure how best to broach the subject.

"How long have you been at Lang Downs?" he settled for asking Harris.

"Since the beginning of the season. I heard a rumor about the bosses and figured this might be a better place for me than some of the other stations I'd worked at," Harris said.

"And has it?" Jeremy asked curiously.

Harris slanted his eyes in Simms's direction. "You could say that. Caine offered to keep me on year-round."

Jeremy nodded. "Lang Downs has always been a place people stayed." The same had never been true of Taylor Peak, much to Jeremy's father's and Devlin's dismay, but that only made the current situation even stranger.

They reached the mob then, and Jeremy didn't have time to ponder the situation anymore. He was too busy calling orders to Arrow and trying to stay out of the way of the others. Harris had a good command of the situation, but some of the men were better at following orders than others.

Between him, Arrow, and Jeremy himself, they got the mob moving back toward the valley. If Jeremy had to send Arrow after more strays than usual, he kept his comments to himself. Harris voiced them for him, and he was the one in charge of the drive, so better for it to come from him.

They got the sheep into the valley and delivered to the breeding pens. Macklin had that down to a science, a kid Jeremy didn't know separating the sheep out one by one and directing them according to Macklin's nods. "Who's that with the boss?" Jeremy asked.

"Jason Thompson. His dad is the head mechanic. He's lived here since he was two. He's got a way with the animals. I thought Seth was supposed to be helping today too. I hope he hasn't skivved off somewhere."

"Seth?"

"Chris's kid brother. Usually you can't keep him and Jason apart unless Seth's working with Patrick, Jason's dad, but Patrick took the weekly run to town for supplies this morning."

"Maybe Macklin sent him to do something else?" Jeremy didn't claim to understand the tone of Harris's voice, but he figured the kid deserved a chance to defend himself before he got reamed for shirking his duties.

"Maybe. He's gotten better, but he played some pranks when he first got here, mostly on his brother, but I won't let him jeopardize Chris's place on the station. We've worked too hard for that."

Before Jeremy could decide how to reply to that, another teenager, a little older than Jason, came running back toward the pens. "Seth will be out in a few minutes, Macklin. He said to tell you he's almost done in the office."

"There, see? A perfectly reasonable explanation."

"Good thing too. Let's get the horses turned out and see what else the boss needs us to do."

Behind them, one of the jackaroos muttered something under his breath. Harris spun on his heel. "You got a problem with working a full day for your pay, Jenkins?"

The man flushed but didn't say anything.

"What's the deal?" Jeremy asked after the man had slunk away. "It's been a while since I've been here, and I never worked here, but I don't remember this kind of attitude."

"It's not all of them," Harris said, "and Jenkins is the worst, by far, but I think the rumors hurt the station when it came to some of their seasonal men. They had to hire people they wouldn't have looked twice at in the past. Some of them, a lot of them, really, have stepped up to do their jobs, but a few of them haven't even tried to learn what they were supposed to do."

"I didn't realize it had gotten that bad," Jeremy said with a shake of his head. "Did they lose any year-rounders?"

"I don't think so," Harris said, "but this was my first season, so I don't know who was here before. The only empty house when I came seemed to be the foreman's house, though, and Neil and Molly have moved into that now. Macklin offered Neil's old house to Chris and Seth, well, and me, I guess, by extension."

That explained the looks he'd seen pass between the two men off and on all day as well as Harris's attitude toward the younger Simms brother. "Hopefully next year will be better," Jeremy said.

"Yeah, and if it's not, at least we'll be expecting it and can plan to deal with it better."

FOUR

JEREMY had just sat down at one of the empty tables in the canteen when Harris walked up and plonked his plate down across from him. "You sitting over here by yourself for a reason?"

Jeremy shrugged. "Emery's pretty much poisoned the year-rounders against me, and the seasonal jackaroos all know each other already. Didn't seem like there was anywhere else to sit."

"Neil's really not that bad once you get to know him," Harris said. "I've heard stories of what he was like when he first found out about Caine, but he's come around. He's never given Chris and me a moment's grief, and he shuts down anyone who tries to say anything about Caine and Macklin before they can say more than the second word."

"That isn't why he hates me," Jeremy said. "My brother owns Taylor Peak—you knew that, right?" Harris nodded. "My father and Old Man Lang were good neighbors. Not good friends, probably, but good neighbors, but then my dad died and Devlin took over. Lang offered his condolences, his help, anything Devlin needed, out of respect for my father and their long-standing acquaintance, but Devlin refused. He said Lang was soft, that he was old-fashioned, and that he was irresponsible on top of that since he'd never married. What would happen to the land when he died?"

"Caine," Harris said with a chuckle.

"Yes, but we didn't know about him at the time. We were neighbors, but we didn't know a lot about his family, nothing about a niece in the US, much less a great-nephew. Anyway, after a while, that irresponsible bit changed. Devlin decided he'd buy the property. He made an offer and Lang rejected him. That might have been the end of it, except Devlin couldn't leave well enough alone. To hear him tell it, Lang insulted him, said he'd burn the place to the ground before he'd sell to Devlin. I find that hard to believe. Mr. Lang was a lot of things, including a hard enough man to carve this place out of nothing, but he wasn't cruel. Not that I've ever seen or heard."

"That's certainly not the impression I got of him from the people here who knew him," Harris agreed. "He's somewhere between a saint and a minor deity to the men who worked with him."

"I'd guess the reality is somewhere in between," Jeremy said. "It usually is when you've got that kind of difference of opinion, but it doesn't matter what Lang actually said to Devlin. Devlin was even more determined to buy Lang Downs. And then Caine came. Devlin approached Macklin when we first heard the station had passed to a relative in the US. He thought he could convince Macklin to use his position as foreman to influence the relative's decisions. I have a suspicion Macklin did just that, only to convince Caine not to sell to Devlin instead of the other way around. That was already bad enough. Then word got around that Caine was gay, and he got intolerable. He called Caine every name you could imagine and set about spreading as many rumors as he could. When he found out about Macklin as well... well, you can imagine the explosion that caused."

Harris shook his head. "Don't think I want to."

"I won't say all the problems you've had this year are Devlin's fault. Someone said enough that Devlin heard about it in the first place, but I know he hasn't made it easier either," Jeremy said, "and the year-rounders have to know that even if it's more guess than fact. I knew I'd have an uphill battle if I came here, but I came anyway because it's still better than anywhere else I might go."

"It is that," Harris replied. "This is the ninth station I've worked on. None of the others have come even close to the sense of belonging here. I'm not saying it'll be easy, with all the bad blood between the stations, but unless there's something you haven't told me, you weren't directly involved. And if that's the case, you can carve a place for yourself here just like Chris and I have done."

Jeremy pondered that for a moment. He'd accepted that he'd burned his bridges with Devlin when he left the way he did. Devlin would probably take him back if he toed the line and got married, but Jeremy didn't intend to do that, certainly not unless gay marriage was legalized at some point, and that wouldn't help his cause with Devlin anyway. He'd come to Lang Downs because he'd known Macklin would take him in for a few days without question. He'd hoped more might come of it, but it had seemed a slim hope at best, and the near fight with Emery hadn't helped change that opinion. Today had been different, though. Today he'd felt like part of the crew, like he actually had something to contribute to the station. Lang Downs might or might not need an extra hand over the winter, but they certainly needed the help now—help Jeremy was well qualified to give.

"Maybe I will," he said with a smile.

"Finish your supper," Harris ordered. "Patrick should be back with the supplies, and that means Chris and I have beer again. You should come have one with us."

"Are you sure?" Jeremy asked. "I wouldn't want to impose."

"I wouldn't have offered if I didn't mean it," Harris—Jeremy supposed he ought to start thinking of the man as Jesse if he was going to drink his beer—replied, standing up. "It's the house closest to the bunkhouse. We'll be up for a couple of hours if you change your mind."

"Nothing to change," Jeremy said quickly. "I'd love to have a beer with you."

"HOW did it go?" Neil asked, sitting down next to Sam at the table.

Sam grinned. "I got the job."

"I knew you would," Neil said with an answering smile. He sobered for a moment. "Is it what you want?"

"Maybe not forever," Sam replied honestly. "It's not something I ever thought about, you know? I never considered moving out of the city. This is nearly as foreign to me as moving to the States would be. That said, I really enjoyed working with Caine today, and it's not like I have a lot of other offers. At least this way I can get my feet back under me. If I look for another job in six months or a year, I'll be doing it with a fresh job on my resume, not with more than a year of unemployment as the top entry."

"Yeah, always a good thing."

"Are you going to be okay with me staying with you?" Sam asked. "I didn't know it would turn into a long-term thing when I asked if I could come."

"There aren't a lot of other options," Neil said. "The foreman's house was only empty because Macklin moved into the big house. Otherwise you'd be crammed into one of the bachelor houses with Molly and me both. I mean, I guess you could move into the bunkhouse when the seasonal jackaroos leave in a couple of weeks, but that's hardly comfortable for more than a season."

"Maybe not, but in a season, maybe other options will open up," Sam said. "You and Molly deserve your privacy, not to mention you might need that guest room for a nursery one of these days."

"Eventually, maybe," Neil said, "but we aren't planning on starting a family right away. We want some time to be together just as a couple first."

"Speaking of which, how are the plans coming?" Sam asked.

"Molly wants to go to Yass in a couple of weeks, after the breeding's done, to look at places for the reception," Neil said. "Once we do that, we can start making other plans. I don't know why we don't just have it here on the station. Caine would let us use the canteen. And there will be plenty of space in the bunkhouse in the middle of winter if people want to come and stay overnight after the ceremony. You should have seen the Christmas party we had. Caine's mother even talked Macklin into dancing."

"With her or with Caine?" Sam asked.

"Both," Neil said. "I couldn't believe it, but everyone clapped and cheered."

"You couldn't believe they danced or that everyone clapped?"

"Mostly that they danced," Neil said. "They keep their affection for each other pretty tightly under wraps when the rest of the men are around, even the year-rounders whose loyalty isn't in question."

"Why?" Sam asked. "I mean, I can understand why they might not want to be obvious in town, but here on the station? It's not like it's a secret."

"You'd have to ask them," Neil said, "but I think some of it is professionalism, some of it is Macklin being an incredibly private person, and some of it is not wanting to make other people uncomfortable in what is their home for the summer."

"I get the professionalism and the being private, but what about them being comfortable in their home?"

"Like I said, that would be a question for them," Neil said, "but Molly and I aren't terribly demonstrative during the day either. I mean, I don't go around kissing her in the canteen or out by the sheds. It's just not the right place for it."

Sam nodded. "Yeah, I guess that's true."

"But the Christmas party was just that," Neil said. "A party. The expectations were different. It was the first time since Caine's arrival that had happened."

"Has it happened since then?"

"Maybe Seth's birthday party," Neil replied after a moment. "It wasn't exactly the same. Nobody was dancing, but it was a party and the atmosphere was much lighter than a typical dinner. Come to think of it, I did see Macklin standing with his arm around Caine. Is there a reason this is so important to you?"

"Trying to figure out how to fit in," Sam said with a shrug. "I don't know how long I'll be here, but who knows? Maybe I'll meet someone someday and want to bring him back here with me. Maybe I'll even meet someone here, not necessarily this winter, but next season maybe there will be someone for me, like you met Molly."

"You never know," Neil said. "It happened to Chris and Jesse. So I guess the answer is for you to watch them and to watch Caine and Macklin. That should give you some sense of how to go on."

"SO WE have a new office manager?" Macklin asked Caine as they got ready for bed that evening.

"We do," Caine said. "By counting room and board as part of his salary, we don't have to pay him as much in cash, and having someone who's actually familiar with Aussie laws will almost certainly save us money in the long run. And we had a good season, even being shorthanded. We sold a record number of lambs and had minimal attrition among the breeding ewes. We'll have all the wool in the spring plus the new lambs. We'll be fine."

"And hopefully next season we'll have a better group of hands," Macklin agreed.

"Even if the same ones come back, they'll know more when they start than they did this spring," Caine said. "And with Jesse familiar with the station now, he'll be able to step up as a crew boss instead of just another jackaroo."

"Jeremy has the experience as well," Macklin said, "although he may not be quite as familiar with the precise lay of the land."

"It won't take him long to learn that," Caine said. "If we make a point of sending him out with whatever crews go out over the winter, he'll know the station well enough by spring."

"We're going to have to keep an eye on Neil," Macklin warned. "He's a hothead and Jeremy is from Taylor Peak."

"I thought the tension was between Devlin and Uncle Michael," Caine said. "And then between Devlin and us."

"It is," Macklin replied, "but Neil sees the name Taylor and won't look any farther. You know how he is."

Caine did indeed know. He'd had the same problem with Neil seeing only the label "gay" and not the rest of Caine's merits when he first found out about Caine. "I'd like to hope it won't come to

Jeremy having to save Neil's life to get him to reconsider his position."

"We'll hope not, although Jeremy being gay won't help any."

"I wasn't planning on telling Neil that part," Caine said with a grin.

"I wasn't either, but I don't know how long Jeremy will want to keep it a secret," Macklin said. "I overheard conversations between some of the seasonal jackaroos about hooking up on their nights off. Now that they aren't afraid of losing their jobs for being gay, they're more open about it than they ever would have been before—here or anywhere else. Jeremy's unattached and attractive, and who knows how long it's been since he last made a trip to town? He might decide to take advantage of the opportunity while he can, and really, why shouldn't he as long as he gets his work done?"

That was news to Caine, but then he tried to stay out of the bunkhouse as much as possible. He wanted the jackaroos to feel like they had their own space where they could relax without the boss hanging over their shoulders constantly.

"As long as the work's done, what they do on their own time is up to them," Caine agreed. "I was thinking we should take a trip for a few days this winter."

"Did you have somewhere in mind?" Macklin asked, seemingly unfazed by the sudden change of subject.

"Well, I've already been to Sydney, so not there," Caine said. "Where's your favorite place in Australia?"

"We're sitting in it."

The words warmed Caine all the way through, but they didn't help. "Your favorite place outside of Lang Downs."

"I don't know," Macklin said. "I haven't really traveled all that much. I ended up here at sixteen and haven't really left except for my yearly trip to Sydney."

"Well, where did you live before you came here?" Caine said, giving up on being discreet. "It could be fun to visit your hometown."

"There is nothing in Tumut that I have any desire to revisit," Macklin said in a flat voice. Caine nodded but inside, he was jumping with delight. He had the name of Macklin's hometown now. He might not get Macklin to go back there, but it gave him a place to start his search. Macklin had lived there until he was fifteen. Even if his family was no longer there, Caine ought to be able to find some record of him.

"Okay, so where's somewhere you've always wanted to go?" Caine asked. If he gave up on the vacation idea that quickly, Macklin would suspect something, and Caine didn't want that. If he wasn't successful or if he didn't find good news, he didn't want Macklin to be disappointed.

"Perth," Macklin said.

"We can look into that," Caine said. "What do you think?"

Macklin shrugged. "No harm in looking, I suppose. I'm just not much of a traveler. I only went to Sydney all those years because Michael insisted."

"My homebody," Caine said with a smile. "Come to bed now?"

Macklin shot him a wolfish smile as he pulled off his thick shirt. Caine leaned back against the pillows and prepared to enjoy the show.

FIVE

SAM looked around the canteen, trying to decide where to sit. With the breeding finished, three weeks into his tenure on the station, the seasonal jackaroos would be leaving in the morning. Kami had broken out the barbie and grilled up more meat than Sam figured three times as many people could eat, along with more sides than Sam knew what to do with. Everyone was in high spirits, the emotion rubbing off even on Sam, but that didn't solve his current problem. Molly and Neil had left for Yass as soon as Macklin declared the work done for the day so they could look at venues for their wedding and reception, leaving Sam with no one he really knew. He'd spent the days working in the office and the evenings with Neil and Molly, or else alone in his room if the other two seemed to want some privacy. He'd gotten a lot of work done, which was good, but he hadn't made any new friends beyond his soon-to-be sister-in-law.

"Don't stand there blocking the food. Come sit down." Sam couldn't remember the name of the kid who spoke, but he followed him back to the table where he was sitting with another kid, two jackaroos… and Jeremy Taylor.

"I'm Jason, by the way," the kid said. "I don't think we've been properly introduced."

"Sam," he said automatically. "Sam Emery. So what do you do on the station?"

"My dad's the head mechanic," Jason said, "but I don't really like engines. I'd much rather work with the animals. Macklin lets me help out some now that I'm old enough. I'm going to be a vet some day and come back here and take care of all the animals."

"How can you not like engines?" the other kid interrupted. From the look on both boys' faces, it was a familiar argument.

"And just like that, we won't get another word out of them tonight not related to the merits of engines versus animals. I'm Chris. That's my brother, Seth. This is Jesse and Jeremy."

"Nice to officially meet you all," Sam said. "I'm Sam, Neil's brother, and I guess Caine's office manager, at least until we can get everything straightened out with the inheritance taxes and everything. I don't know if he'll need me after that."

"He'd rather be out with Macklin on the station," Jesse said. "As long as you're willing to put up with the station and the job, he'll keep you around."

"Why wouldn't I?" Sam asked.

"Because a lot of people think life on a station is all romantic, like you see in the movies," Jeremy answered before Jesse could, "when really it's a lot of isolation and hard work, extremes of temperature, and the weather trying to beat the shit out of you. There's nothing romantic about life on a station."

Chris and Jesse snickered.

"I didn't say you couldn't have a romance on a station," Jeremy said, rolling his eyes, "because that obviously happens. We've got three couples on this station right now who met here, and that's just the ones I know about. That's not what I mean. I mean the way it's portrayed in movies. We saw it every year at Taylor Peak. We'd hire on these young guys, all fresh-faced and convinced they were setting off on some grand adventure. Half of them didn't even make it through a single season, much less come back."

"I'm not working under any illusions," Sam said, "but I have a roof over my head, food to eat, and a job that uses my skills. That's a little hard to complain about."

"We'll see what you say in the middle of July, when it's freezing cold, or in the middle of December when it's so hot you can barely breathe," Jeremy said.

"That sounds like a challenge to me," Sam said, not quite believing his own temerity. "What do I get if I make it? If I last a year?"

"All the beer you want for a year," Jeremy replied without batting an eyelash. "If you make it through April of next year, I'll buy you beer for a year."

"Deal," Sam said, holding out his hand to shake on it.

Jeremy sealed the deal, and if Sam didn't pull his hand back as quickly as he might once have done, no one seemed at all bothered by it.

"I asked Macklin if I could take the supply run tomorrow," Jeremy said, changing the subject completely. "Anybody need anything while I'm in town?"

"I could use a couple of things," Chris said. "I'll make you a list."

"No, I'm good," Jesse said.

"Do you think I could come with you?" Sam asked. "I don't have much of anything I'll need for the winter up here, but boots and coats aren't something I can ask someone else to buy for me."

"There's an extra seat in the ute," Jeremy said with a shrug. "The drive'll go faster with someone to talk to."

It wasn't as enthusiastic a response as Sam might have hoped, but it was better than a refusal. Sam reminded himself Jeremy had a history with Neil, even if Sam didn't know the details, and that of course Jeremy would be cautious since he didn't know if Sam would share Neil's opinions. "Thanks. What time are you planning on leaving?"

"As soon as we're done with breakfast," Jeremy replied. "It's a four-hour drive to Boorowa."

"I'll be ready."

Caine stood up at the front of the room and whistled for everyone's attention before they could say anything else.

"I want to thank everyone for their hard work this season," he began. "None of you had to take a chance on Lang Downs when we hired you in the spring, whether this was your first season on the station or another of many. None of you had to take a chance on me. This year could have been a disaster for us. New owner, a lot of new men, but it wasn't, and that's due to your hard work, particularly Neil, Kyle, and Ian, who worked harder than I would have asked of anyone. We had a good summer, and you'll all find a little something extra in your final paycheck in the morning. I wish you all the best this winter and look forward to seeing you again next spring."

The jackaroos all applauded at the news of a bonus.

"He's too generous," Jesse muttered. "Half of them barely even earned their actual paycheck, much less a bonus."

"He can afford to be generous," Sam said. "Whether they deserve it or not, the station is in the black."

"That's good news," Jeremy said. "I don't know if this was truth or Devlin being a bastard, but I heard rumors the station had a rough year before Lang died, maybe even a rough couple of years."

Sam didn't say anything since he wasn't sure how much Caine was comfortable sharing with his employees, but it hadn't just been rumors. The numbers hadn't been bad enough to put the station in danger, but Sam had seen a couple of years in the red as he'd looked back through the accounts to get a sense of trends. Weather and circumstances beyond the graziers' control had played into that, Sam knew, but Caine had turned it around. He and Macklin were a formidable team.

Jeremy grinned. "Of course, knowing Devlin, he probably made it all up to deflect attention from the issues Taylor Peak was having at the same time."

"Mismanagement aside, I would think weather conditions and that sort of thing would affect both stations fairly equally," Sam said. "I mean, it's not like they're on opposite sides of the territory. They're neighbors."

"Yes, much to my brother's dismay," Jeremy said. "I, on the other hand, think it's bloody brilliant."

"Why's that?" Sam asked.

"Because anything that annoys my brother is bloody brilliant in my book," Jeremy replied. "He's a misogynistic, racist, homophobic bigot, and I'm done defending him, no matter what *your* brother thinks. He didn't like it when I told him that, but I'm done with him, so it doesn't matter."

Sam noticed the nearly faded bruise around Jeremy's eye, the slight discoloration mostly hidden by his tanned skin. "That how you got the black eye?"

"I might have said a few things he didn't like," Jeremy said. "It was worth it, though, and he looked worse than I did when I was done with him."

Sam took a moment to be grateful to Caine for changing Neil's homophobic attitude before Sam arrived. Without that, Sam could all too easily imagine them coming to blows, only Sam wouldn't have acquitted himself nearly as well as Jeremy seemed to have done. Sam's strength had always been numbers, not fists.

SAM lay in bed that night and replayed the conversation with Jeremy, and the easy way he accepted Jesse and Chris. Sam hadn't noticed anything in their behavior right away, but it had become more obvious over the course of the evening. Jeremy hadn't even blinked when Seth had made an obnoxious adolescent comment about how close they were sitting together and nobody wanting to see that. Jesse had casually smacked the teen on the back of the head, and everyone, Seth included, had laughed. If anything, Chris and Jesse had sat even closer after that.

Not being homophobic didn't make Jeremy gay, though, and that was what Sam found himself wishing could be true. He had taken to observing the jackaroos in the canteen since he arrived, and already he could tell the difference between the year-rounders and the seasonal ones. They moved differently, looked different, carried themselves with a different kind of confidence, like somehow the land beneath their feet grounded them in a way it didn't do for the seasonal employees.

Jeremy had arrived on Lang Downs the same day Sam had, but Jeremy moved the same way Neil and Macklin did, with the innate grace and confidence that came from knowing what they were doing and knowing they could handle anything the tablelands threw at them. Sam found it insanely attractive.

Of course even if Jeremy was gay, he'd never look twice at someone like Sam, who didn't know the first thing about sheep and probably wouldn't last an hour without doing something stupid.

It wouldn't stop him from looking, though, or from fantasizing occasionally. He'd hooked up with some attractive men over the past year, but none of them held a candle to Jeremy's ruggedness. He had lines around his eyes from squinting against the sun and a scar on his cheek, long since healed. He wasn't classically handsome by any stretch of the imagination, but Sam had seen the wicked sense of humor in his blue-green eyes, the way they came alive as he told tale after tale of growing up on a sheep station and all the antics of a teenaged boy. He'd run his fingers through his short blond hair at one point, leaving it in spiky disarray. Sam figured that would be enough to feed his dreams for weeks, because unlike the men he'd hooked up with or the ones he'd watched furtively on porn sites, Jeremy was for real.

It would be easy to beat off right now to the memory of laughing eyes, mussed hair, and a crooked smile, but the alarm would go off early, and when it did, Sam would get to spend the entire day with Jeremy. That was far better than an empty fantasy. With that thought in mind, he rolled onto his side and willed himself to sleep.

JEREMY was actually surprised to see Sam at breakfast the next morning. The seasonal jackaroos, the ones who had worked their last day the day before, had all taken the excuse to sleep in, and even some of the year-rounders hadn't made it up. If Lang Downs was anything like Taylor Peak, things were a little more relaxed in the winter, with less to do during the shorter days, so it wasn't that much of a stretch. Sam, though, was in the same seat he'd been in every morning since his arrival at Lang Downs. Jeremy pretended he hadn't noticed, but he couldn't help himself.

Sam Emery was everything Jeremy wasn't: controlled, polished, slick in a way Jeremy could never hope to be. Jeremy figured Sam could blend in at any business anywhere in the country, just walk into the office and start running the place. Jeremy hadn't seen him in a suit yet—not exactly the kind of thing one wore on a sheep station—but even his casual clothes had a look about them that said he was used to wearing good clothes.

He knew what Devlin would say about someone like Sam, calling him a blow-in or worse, making fun of him for his "city ways" and his inability to blend in on the station, but from what Jeremy could see, no one at Lang Downs had received Sam that way. It helped that he wasn't pretending to be a jackaroo. He'd come for a visit and then stayed, working in the big house on the accounts for the station. Jeremy had learned a lot of things at uni, studying animal management, but accounting hadn't been one of them. He had a head for animals, not numbers, so he had the utmost respect for anyone who could manage the complexities of a station's financials.

It didn't hurt either that Sam was good-looking. Unlike most of the men Jeremy was used to seeing on the station, Sam actually looked like he'd been inside a barbershop in the past ten years. His dark hair was parted neatly and combed straight without any pretension, but Jeremy thought it fit him, fit the whole put-together thing Sam had going on. He had a high forehead, but that worked with the square jaw and strong chin. The only thing that threw off the impression of strength was the self-effacing expression Sam had worn every time Jeremy had laid eyes on him, like he was used to people looking right past him without even a second glance. Jeremy didn't know what the hell was wrong with people if that was the treatment Sam had gotten used to, because Jeremy had a hard time looking away. With his luck, though, Sam was straight. Jeremy didn't claim to have the most developed gaydar, but he wasn't getting any vibes off Sam at all.

Of course he'd barely talked to the man, which might have something to do with it. He hadn't approached, despite his attraction, when Sam was with Emery. He'd told Macklin he wouldn't start anything with his right-hand man, and he'd meant it. Unfortunately that had made talking to Sam difficult because Sam was almost always with his brother. He'd practically sent Jason to get Sam last night when he'd realized Emery and his fiancée were gone for a few days, and the conversation had been light and easy, with Sam displaying none of the intolerance toward Chris and Jesse that Emery had reputedly shown toward Caine when he'd first found out Caine was gay. Jeremy took that as a good sign, but it didn't mean anything more than Sam being more open-minded than his brother. Personally, Jeremy didn't think that would be hard to do.

"Jeremy?"

Jeremy looked up at the sound of his name to see Sam standing on the other side of the table from where Jeremy sat. "Hi, g'morning. Let me just finish my coffee and we can go."

"No rush," Sam said. "I just wanted to let you know I was ready whenever you were. You did say you wanted to get an early start."

"No, it's fine. I'm done eating. I was just enjoying my coffee for a minute. It's not many mornings we get to do that."

"No, I'm getting that impression," Sam said, taking the seat across from Jeremy. "I can always get another cup for us both if you want one. We can enjoy the quiet."

"Why don't you get us both a cup to go?" Jeremy suggested. "There will be plenty of quiet in the ute, and it's getting cold too. The coffee will keep us warm until the heater kicks in."

Sam smiled and walked toward the kitchen for more coffee. "Smooth, Taylor," Jeremy muttered. "Real bloody smooth."

He gulped the last few mouthfuls of his cooling coffee and pushed back from the table as Sam reappeared from the kitchen, a thermos and two tin cups in hand. "All set."

"Me too," Jeremy said. "Macklin gave me the keys last night, and Paul in Boorowa has the station's order already."

"Yes, I saw the bill come in from last month," Sam said. "It seems like there's a standing order, at least for summer."

"That's the way we did it at Taylor Peak," Jeremy confirmed as they climbed into the ute and started across Lang Downs. "Devlin had a regular order on file with Paul, and then he'd call the day before and update it if we needed anything extra or different than usual."

"And if you needed less?"

"That never happened. Devlin always ordered just a little less than he thought we'd need so there wouldn't be any waste. Everyone hated Fridays and almost all the jackaroos went to town on Saturdays. Devlin counted it as a win because then he didn't have to feed them."

"That's...."

"You can say it," Jeremy said. "He's my brother, but we don't have the same kind of relationship you have with your brother. He's a tightwad and more than a bit of a bastard at the best of times."

"Is that why you left?" Sam asked.

"That's part of it," Jeremy said. "I got tired of listening to him, of him thinking he could run my life. I figured I'd throw myself on Macklin's mercy for a few days. I didn't expect him to offer me a job."

Sam laughed. "Yeah, I know that feeling. I called Neil, needing a place to stay for a few days while I sorted things out with my ex-wife. I didn't expect it to turn into a job offer."

Ex-wife. Jeremy's stomach clenched with disappointment. That was that, then. Sam wasn't gay.

"Sorry to hear about the divorce," he said automatically.

"Don't be," Sam replied. "Yeah, it hurts to admit the marriage failed, but honestly, we're both better off this way. We weren't right for each other. I'll never be what she wanted, and she wasn't ever what I wanted. I married her to appease my old man."

"He gone now?" Jeremy understood the weight of familial expectation even if he'd always managed to resist it. He and Sam had more in common than it had first appeared.

"Yeah, he's been gone for a couple of years. We were still bumping along then, but I lost my job a year and a half ago, and that was pretty much the end. It just took us a few months to realize it. When she asked for a separation and then a divorce, I didn't fight it."

SIX

SAM was surprised how quickly the drive to Boorowa seemed to go. He had been a little nervous about all that time in the ute with Jeremy, since he barely knew the other man, but they'd chatted easily the entire time, mostly about the station and what to expect over the winter. Jeremy had been a font of information, taking the time to answer all Sam's questions with more patience than Neil had shown the few times Sam had tried to ask him about the coming months.

"Thanks for being so patient with all my questions," Sam said as they reached the main road into Boorowa. "Neil forgets I don't have his experience."

"No offense to your brother, because he's a fantastic jackaroo, but he's got some things to learn about managing people if he's going to work as Macklin's foreman," Jeremy said. "There's a lot more to it than just giving orders."

"He's never had a lot of patience with what he considers stupid questions," Sam admitted. "The problem is he's never really figured out that they aren't stupid questions to the person asking them. Besides, it's not like Macklin is planning on retiring anytime soon, at least not from the impression Caine gave me."

"Oh, I'm sure he's not," Jeremy said. "He's just like my father and Mr. Lang. He'll die working that station rather than retire from it, but he's not just the foreman now. He's the boss, and sometimes it helps to have a layer between the boss and the jackaroos. It shouldn't make any difference. The orders still come from the boss regardless of who gives them, but I've seen it year after year. It might take Macklin a season or two to get used to the idea, but he'll see it before long. Your brother is the most logical candidate, but he's not the only one, and if he wants the job, he's going to have to figure out how to explain things to the blow-ins without making them reconsider their decision to work on the station."

"I'll mention it to him," Neil said.

"Don't tell him I gave you the advice," Jeremy warned. "He'll ignore it out of spite."

"What's that all about, anyway?" Sam asked.

Jeremy shrugged. "Blaming me for my brother's idiocy. Devlin has made some enemies on Lang Downs, but I'm not my brother, something your brother doesn't seem interested in acknowledging."

"Yeah, he gets that way sometimes," Sam apologized. "I could talk to him, try to get him to see that whatever happened wasn't your fault."

"Cheers, mate, but don't put yourself out. I don't want to make problems between you over something that isn't your problem in the first place. He'll get used to seeing me around and maybe one of these days he'll realize I'm not Devlin, and I don't share his opinions about Caine or about how to run a station."

"Which of those is the real problem?" Sam asked. "Because you know he would have shared your brother's opinion about Caine until a year or so ago."

"Which opinion?" Jeremy asked. "That he was a blow-in with no business owning a station or that he was an embarrassment to us all because he's a poofter?"

Sam cringed a little hearing the insult fall casually from Jeremy's mouth. "Both, probably," Sam admitted, "although he seems to have gotten over both. Caine saved his life. I don't know if you knew that part. Neil's loyal to him now."

"I'd heard it mentioned," Jeremy said. "For what it's worth, I think it's bloody brilliant that we have some new blood around here to shake things up, and what Caine does in his private life and with who is none of my business. I told you, I don't share Devlin's opinions."

"That's good to hear since you're working for him now," Sam said.

"I wouldn't have accepted Macklin's offer if I couldn't work here in good conscience," Jeremy said. "Neil thinks I'm here to undermine the station or something ridiculous like that, but I'm not. I had a falling out with my brother and coming here was the easiest option open to me. If it hadn't worked out, I would have gone elsewhere, but it did, and I'm not about to complain about working with a man I respect, doing a job I love."

"You sound just like Neil. That's what makes it so bloody stupid that he won't see past your name."

"Prejudices are tricky things," Jeremy replied philosophically. "It takes a lot to make a person see past them sometimes. I meant what I told Macklin that first night. I won't start anything with Neil. I'll work with a different team or do something else entirely. I don't need to be foreman or in charge of a team or anything else. I'm happy with a roof over my head and Kami's excellent cooking. Neil will see that eventually or he won't, but it's no skin off my back either way."

Sam wasn't sure why it was so important to him that Neil and Jeremy reach a point of tolerating each other—or rather, that Neil reach a point of tolerating Jeremy—but the station was a small place, about to get smaller with all the seasonal jackaroos leaving for the winter, and no one wanted to live with that kind of tension between coworkers.

He deliberately pushed aside thoughts of his own interest in Jeremy. He had no reason to believe that was reciprocated, and he didn't want to add tension of his own to the mix.

"Speaking of a roof over your head," Sam said, "you'll be the only one in the bunkhouse after today, right?"

"Yeah, that's right. Why?"

"Because I can only spend so many nights listening to Neil and Molly without wanting to strangle them or smother myself," Sam said with a wry smile, "and there aren't a lot of other empty beds on the station except in the bunkhouse. Caine mentioned the spare room in the big house, but when I mentioned that, Chris started laughing, so I suspect it wouldn't be any quieter than my current room." And a lot harder to ignore. Sam would never impinge on a relationship like that, but the thought of Caine and Macklin together did a hell of a lot more to his libido than the thought of Neil and Molly. "I'd like to get a full night's sleep again one of these days."

"Once the jackaroos clear out, you're welcome to whichever room you want, as far as I'm concerned," Jeremy said. "It'll be nice to have someone to share all that space with. Nights can get lonely out here without someone to talk to or share a beer with."

"Brilliant," Sam said. "I'll get moved in when we get back tonight."

"You don't want to stay in Boorowa tonight?" Jeremy asked. "They won't expect us to make the return trip today."

Sam's face fell as he mentally revised his spending plans for the day. "I hadn't planned on it," he admitted. "I guess I didn't think it through. I'm not sure I have enough to pay for a hotel room and new gear. I guess I'll have to get a few things this month and come back next month to buy more."

"I didn't mean to put you on the spot," Jeremy apologized immediately. "I forgot this was your first check. This time of year, most people are flush from a summer's wages and nowhere to really spend them. We'll just shop fast and drive late to get back. I know Taylor Peak well enough to drive across it even at night, and once we get back on Lang Downs, the roads are maintained enough to follow with no problem."

"Sorry," Sam said. "I didn't mean to mess up your plans for the day. If you want to stay in town, I could sleep in the ute." It would be hell on his back, but it would be better than making Jeremy change his plans because Sam was short on cash.

"No worries," Jeremy said. "That would be cold and miserable. We'll be there in about fifteen minutes. I'll tell Paul we're in a bit of a hurry so he loads everything up quickly. We'll get what you need, get lunch, and get back on the road this afternoon.

We can pick up sandwiches to eat as we drive back since we won't make it home in time for dinner, but we'll get back tonight."

"Thanks," Sam said, not sure he had hidden his relief as much as he wanted to. "Next time, when I don't have to buy a whole new kit, I'll make it up to you."

"There's nothing to make up," Jeremy insisted. "The Boorowa Hotel is nice enough, but it's not like there's tons of things to do in town. It's habit, more than anything else, to stay the night. I know some of the men hook up with the town girls, but that's never been my style."

"Not into casual hookups?" Sam asked.

"I've got nothing against them," Jeremy said, "but I'm not into small-town drama, and in a town this size, there's always something."

Sam remembered how much drama had surrounded his casual hookups in Melbourne, how he'd always checked out the bars he went to, making sure the guy he'd slept with last time wasn't there before he settled down to meet someone new, and the tension he felt if a guy he'd hooked up with before came in while he was still there. The sex had been good. The rest had been more drama than he needed in his life.

"Yeah, I can see that," Sam said when he realized Jeremy seemed to be waiting for a reply. "It's not really my scene either."

"You wouldn't want to give your ex something to drag into court, anyway," Jeremy said. "No reason to make your divorce messier than it has to be."

"I'm not fighting her over anything," Sam said. "I just want it to be done and the papers signed. I'm ready for that part of my life to be over."

"How much longer?" Jeremy asked as they reached the outskirts of Boorowa, if such a term could apply to a town of only about a thousand people.

"No more than six months, I hope," Sam replied. "I'll have to go back to Melbourne to sign off on everything, but since she's keeping everything but my personal belongings, clothes and stuff, it's not like there's anything to haggle over."

"That makes it easier, I guess," Jeremy said, parking the ute near the general store. "Let's see what we can do about getting you sorted. Paul should have everything you need, and if not, he can order it and someone can pick it up on the next trip into town."

"What do you think I'll need?" Sam asked as they walked toward the store. "I figured a pair of boots, a coat, and a few pairs of sturdier pants would be enough to get me through the winter."

"Depends on whether you're spending all your time in the office or if you're going to come out in the paddocks with us," Jeremy said. "If you're in the office all the time, that'll be more than enough. You probably could even do without the sturdier pants just for walking across the main road of the station to the big house. If you're coming out with us, you'll want long underwear and gloves as well as a hat and a Driza-Bone. A shearling coat is fine for keeping you warm on a short walk, but if you're out riding, you'll want the Driza-Bone both because it's waterproof and because it'll protect your legs, as well."

"I don't know," Sam said. "I've never gone riding before, and I'm sure I'd just be in the way."

"Not in the winter," Jeremy said. "Everything is much more laid-back. There's not a lot to do, just keeping tabs on everything. It's actually a really good time to get your feet wet because people have the time to explain and teach instead of having the pressure of the high season on them."

"Are you offering to teach me?" Sam asked, unable to completely stop the shot of anticipation at the thought of spending hours with the sexy jackaroo.

"If you want," Jeremy said, "although I figured you'd prefer to go out with Neil."

Sam shrugged. "It's that whole older brother, younger brother thing. It makes him a bad teacher."

"Then yes, I'll be glad to teach you."

"Good. Then you'll have to make sure I get what I need," Sam said with a huge smile.

They walked into the store, and Jeremy called out a greeting to the store owner.

"What are you doing here today, Jeremy?" the man called back. "I don't have an order for Taylor Peak to pick up until Tuesday."

"I'm not here for Taylor Peak's order, Paul," Jeremy said. "I'm here for Lang Downs's order, and to pick up a few things for myself and my friend."

"Does your brother know where you're living?" Paul asked.

"I don't know, and what's more, I don't care," Jeremy replied. "He made his opinions clear when he ordered me off the station. We're going to drive back tonight, so if you can get the order ready to load as quickly as possible, we'd appreciate it."

Paul pursed his lips like he had something to say still, but whatever it was, he held his tongue, and Jeremy let it go, ushering Sam toward the back where Paul had shirts, work pants, and long underwear stacked. "I'll let you dig through and find your own size," he said to Sam. "I've got to get a few things of my own."

Sam let him go. He wanted help picking out the right boots, hat, and jacket, but he could pick out his own trousers and shirts. The selection wasn't anything fancy, but Sam didn't need fancy. He had fancy already. The problem was what he didn't have. He picked out three pairs of trousers and three shirts. He'd have to do laundry or else wear his city clothes when he was only going to be in the office, but he had a budget, and he had other things to buy as well.

He set the things he'd selected on the counter and went to find Jeremy. "So what kind of boots should I get?"

"I like Blundstones, although R.M. Williams is a good brand too," Jeremy said. "I think Paul has both, so you can try them on and see which one fits you best."

Sam asked for his size, and Paul came back a few minutes later with a pair of each brand in the right size. Sam toed off his loafers and got ready to try the boots on.

"Wait," Jeremy said. "If you wear them with that kind of socks, you'll tear your feet up." He grabbed a pack of thick cotton socks and tossed them to Sam. "You'll need a pack anyway, so go ahead and take a pair out so you can try the boots on with the right kind of socks."

Feeling like the biggest dunce in the world, Sam did as Jeremy directed and switched his socks for the new pair. They were soft, thick, and so incredibly warm that he took a minute just to relish the feeling. A smothered cough brought him back to the present, and he quickly tried on the first pair of boots.

They were a little snug, so he pulled them off and tried on the second pair. "These are much more comfortable," he said.

"Then get those," Jeremy replied with a smile. He flicked a hat in Sam's direction. "Try that on."

Sam set the hat on his head, adjusting the brim until it settled comfortably. "How does it look?"

"Like it was made to fit you," Jeremy said, his smile widening. Sam told himself to stop acting like a teenager with his first crush, but he couldn't stop the bolt of pleasure that went through him at the compliment and the smile. Jeremy probably didn't mean anything by it, but he was paying attention, and apparently that was all it took to make Sam's heart beat a little faster.

"I know better than that," Sam said, squirming a little under Jeremy's continued stare, "but maybe one day, that'll be true."

"Everyone has to start somewhere," Jeremy said, "and you started somewhere else, in a different life and a different career. There's nothing wrong with that."

Sam had a hard time believing that at the moment, but he knew Jeremy was right. He just had to convince himself of it all over again in the midst of a station full of men whose masculinity was far more overt and physical. When he'd been an office manager in a city full of people with nine-to-five jobs, it had been easier to believe in his own abilities and to see his own worth. Being unable to find a new job had shaken that, but he'd tried not to give up. Coming to Lang Downs had brought him a new job, but it also gave him a whole new standard to live up to, and he was all too aware of the softness of his own body compared to the man standing next to him.

"So, what else do I need? You said something about a coat," Sam said, deflecting Jeremy's attention again.

"A Driza-Bone," Jeremy said. "They're back here."

He led Sam to the back of the store where a rack of long, dark dusters stood. He pulled one off and handed it to Sam. "Try it on, but don't be surprised if it doesn't feel quite right immediately. It has to warm up before it fits right."

Sam slid the coat over his shoulders and twitched a little, trying to get it to settle correctly. It felt distinctly odd after the suit jackets he had grown accustomed to wearing, but he already knew those would be worthless at Lang Downs. "So, what's so special about this kind of coat?" he asked while he waited for his body heat to allow it to settle more comfortably.

"It's waterproof, for one thing," Jeremy said, "but the biggest thing is how it's cut. See the split in the back? When you're riding, that falls on either side of the horse, and you can wrap the tails around your legs to keep them warm and dry as well."

"I've never ridden a horse in my life," Sam said. "Are you sure I need this?"

"I told you I'd teach you about life on a station," Jeremy reminded him. "That means riding, especially in the winter when the weather sometimes makes the roads impassable."

Sam had a bad feeling about this, but he nodded anyway. Maybe he'd end up making a total fool of himself, but it had to be better than not taking the chance at all. If he had any hope of winning the respect of the men he'd be working and living with— not just Jeremy, although that would be nice, but all of them—he had to learn at least the basics of how the station worked. "You do realize what you're getting yourself into, right?"

Jeremy grinned, the expression just wolfish enough to make Sam wonder if maybe Jeremy wasn't as straight as Sam had assumed. "I'm looking forward to it."

Sam gulped and turned his attention back to the Driza-Bone, which had softened around him as they talked. "You know, this is pretty comfortable now that it's warmed up."

"Good," Jeremy said. "Then the only thing left is a pair of heavy gloves. It gets cold up in the tablelands, and you'll want the protection for when we're working too." He grabbed Sam's hand and turned it palm up, then put his own hand next to it. "You've got a few calluses to develop before you'll be comfortable working without them."

"I see that," Sam said, his stomach sinking again. He couldn't think of a single thing a man like Jeremy would see in someone like him. "Guess I better get a pair of gloves, then."

"Hey," Jeremy said as Sam started to turn away. "I wasn't making fun of you. It's like I said. You chose a different career, and that's still your job. All the rest, that's just helping you be a little more comfortable in your new home. Nobody expects you to be a jackaroo. Caine and Macklin hired you to do the station's books, not tend the sheep. Believe me, I'd be as lost doing the accounts as you feel thinking about the stuff I do. I can keep track of anything you want where the animals are concerned, but I had to drop the one business class I took, it was so far over my head."

"Really?" Sam said. "But it's just numbers."

"And tax laws and hiring regulations and a hundred other things like that," Jeremy insisted. "It was a disaster. I stayed as far away from the books at Taylor Peak as I could. Now it's not my problem since I'm just a jackaroo at Lang Downs."

Sam didn't think Jeremy could ever be "just" anything, but he kept that observation to himself. He genuinely liked Jeremy, and he didn't want to lose his friendship by coming onto him until he was sure Jeremy was interested. Sure, he'd gotten a few signals suggesting he might be, but Sam wasn't ready to take that risk just yet. Besides, starting a new relationship before his divorce was final would be asking for trouble when the time came. Not that he could give Alison any more than he'd already agreed to give her, but he could do without the drama.

"So what kind of gloves should I get?" Sam asked. He doubted he'd ever be as comfortable or confident on the station as Jeremy, but he could at least learn enough to take part in the discussions over dinner.

SEVEN

BY THE time they'd finished lunch, Jeremy was glad they'd decided not to stay in town overnight. If he had to answer one more question about what had happened with Devlin and why he was living at Lang Downs now, he thought he might hit someone.

"The curse of small towns," he muttered as they paid for their meal.

"I don't know," Sam said, following Jeremy out of the restaurant. "People know you here. If you were in trouble, you'd have help."

"That's probably true," Jeremy agreed, although he suspected a revelation of his sexuality would impact who and how many would help. Macklin hadn't been completely ostracized, but Jeremy had heard enough disapproving whispers to know some people would turn him away. "But it also means no privacy and no personal boundaries a lot of the time."

They reached the ute and started loading the supplies Paul had gathered for them on the loading dock of the store. By the time they were done, Jeremy had worked up enough of a sweat to roll up his sleeves. He considered taking off his work shirt and driving home in just his T-shirt, but he'd cool off soon enough and wish he'd left it on. "You ready to go?"

Sam nodded mutely, the first time all day he hadn't had a ready answer when Jeremy spoke to him, but Jeremy didn't push. They'd gotten up early and had a busy day, and it was only midafternoon. They had a four-hour drive ahead of them still, possibly more if the clouds that had gathered let loose the threatened storm. Jeremy might cut directly across the paddocks rather than sticking to the roads if the weather was clear, but he wasn't going to risk getting mired on Taylor Peak. He didn't want to have another run-in with Devlin, especially with Sam in tow. Sam didn't deserve to get caught up in the middle of their family dispute.

They headed west out of town back toward the tablelands and the station. A couple of times, Jeremy thought he caught Sam staring at his forearms where the sleeves were still rolled up, but he couldn't be sure, and he didn't want to disturb the easy camaraderie between them by asking. He'd had guys in Sydney or Melbourne fawn over his arms before, but he'd never thought they were anything special, just the product of a lifetime of work on a sheep station, no different than any of the other stockmen around him. Sam wasn't a stockman, though. Of course he also shouldn't have been interested in Jeremy's arms, not unless there was more to the business with the ex-wife than Sam had said.

Jeremy wouldn't blame him for not mentioning it if there was. He hadn't exactly been forthcoming about his own secrets, so he couldn't expect Sam to be any different, if in fact that was what was going on. Or maybe Sam was just staring blindly into space and the most comfortable position for his head happened to be with his eyes in the direction of Jeremy's arms. Jeremy figured that was about as likely as someone like Sam being interested in a stockman from the tablelands.

"It looks like we're in for a storm," Sam said about the time they reached the turn-off for Taylor Peak and Lang Downs.

"Yeah. Let's get through the gate, and then we'd better lash down the tarp over the supplies. If Caine's order is anything like Devlin's, none of it needs to get wet," Jeremy said.

Sam nodded and hopped out to open the gate. Jeremy drove through and parked. He met Sam at the back of the ute and wrestled with the huge tarp. "Before we put this on, you might want to get your Driza-Bone," Jeremy said. "If it starts raining, you'll be glad for it when we get to the gates."

Sam grabbed his coat from the package of his supplies, and then together they got the flatbed of the ute covered and the tarp lashed into place. The wind picked up while they worked, enough to make Jeremy glad of the extra pair of hands. He could have managed on his own, but having Sam's help made it faster and easier.

"Thanks for the help," he said as they climbed back into the ute.

"You're welcome," Sam replied, "not that I really did anything."

Jeremy had noticed Sam's penchant for self-effacement earlier in the day, and there it was again, the assumption that somehow his contributions were less important or less significant than anyone else's. "You held the tarp down against the wind while I tied it in place," Jeremy said. "If you hadn't, I'd have been fighting the wind and the rope instead of just the rope."

"You would have managed."

"Yes," Jeremy said, because he could hardly deny it, "but having your help made it easier."

Sam retreated back into abashed silence, and Jeremy bit back the urge to shout at him. It made him wonder if there wasn't more to Sam's divorce than he'd admitted to. Modesty was one thing; Sam's lack of confidence smacked of emotional abuse.

They were nearing the second gate, the one that would take them to the main house at Taylor Peak or let them bypass it for the road to Lang Downs, when another set of headlights caught Jeremy's eye. "Looks like we have company," he said to Sam.

Next to him, Sam tensed, almost as if he was expecting a blow. "Is there a problem?"

"There shouldn't be," Jeremy said, resisting the urge to pat Sam's knee comfortingly. He didn't know if the gesture would be appreciated, so he kept his hands on the steering wheel and waited for the other vehicle to approach. "The only way to Boorowa from Lang Downs is through Taylor Peak. As long as the jackaroos don't cause problems, we've never had an issue with them crossing our land, and Mr. Lang was always very clear with his men. If you cause problems on Taylor Peak, don't bother coming back. I haven't heard Macklin say anything like that, but I can't imagine he'd be any more tolerant of it."

"He doesn't seem one to bear fools lightly," Sam agreed. "I guess we just wait and see what they want?"

"Yes," Jeremy replied. "It could be nothing at all, but since we've seen them, it's polite to wait and acknowledge them. They'll be here in a minute, and then we can head on home."

A few moments later, the other vehicle came into sight, and Jeremy's stomach fell when he recognized Devlin's car. He rolled down the window on the ute, the cold breeze eddying through the warmth of the cab. He could get out and preserve the warmth, but he really wanted the door between him and his brother. He didn't think they would come to blows again, but he could do without another shiner.

"Jeremy," Devlin said as he approached the ute. "I heard you were in town today."

"I made the supply run for Lang Downs," Jeremy replied, "not that it's any of your business."

"I heard that too," Devlin said. "You're really going to choose those two no-good pillow biters over your own family?"

"If the choice is living with your bigotry or living with Caine and Macklin, I'll be far happier on Lang Downs," Jeremy replied evenly. "I told you that the day I left. I'm done playing by your rules."

"You're no better than they are," Devlin spat. He peered deeper into the ute at Sam. "Bloody hell, if that's the best they can do for jackaroos these days, you've jumped onto a sinking ship."

Jeremy grabbed Devlin's collar in his fist and dragged him close. "Listen, you stupid fucker, you can insult me all day long, but you leave Sam out of it. He's the accountant Caine and Macklin hired to take care of the books because Lang Downs is doing so well they need someone full time, so get it through your bloody thick skull that Lang Downs isn't going under, you're not going to be able to buy it cheap, and you're not going to be able to run Caine off. They're worth ten of you."

"Bloody poofters, the whole lot," Devlin said. "Next thing you know, you'll be joining them too. Don't come running to me when it goes south on you."

"I haven't come running to you for anything since I was five and you laughed at me for falling off my first pony," Jeremy said.

"I should have known there was something wrong with you then," Devlin sneered.

"There's not a thing wrong with me," Jeremy replied, "except how long it took me to tell you to go to hell."

Not waiting for an answer, he rolled up the window and let up on the brake. He didn't gun the engine. He didn't want to hurt Devlin, after all, just get the hell away from him.

"I'm sorry you had to hear that," Jeremy said to Sam after Devlin had stepped back and was nothing more than a shadow in his rearview mirror. "Devlin has a blind spot so wide you could drive a truck through it where Caine and Macklin are concerned. It was bad enough when he thought I agreed with him. Now that he realizes I don't, he's added me to his blacklist."

"It's fine," Sam said in a meek voice. "It's not your fault."

They reached the gate, and Sam jumped out to open it before Jeremy could say anything else. He drove through and waited for Sam to join him again.

"You're not freaking out because you found out I'm gay, are you?" Jeremy asked. "You didn't seem bothered by Caine and Macklin, so I thought—"

"What? No, of course not," Sam said. "That would be really stupid, not to mention hypocritical. I mean, I didn't know until your brother said something, but it's none of my business, and you had no reason to tell me—"

"Sam, breathe," Jeremy interrupted. "You're going to hyperventilate if you keep going like that."

Obediently Sam leaned forward and put his head between his knees, breathing in slow, measured cadence. Jeremy might have chuckled at the sight if he hadn't been so busy resisting the urge to plant a fist in the face of whoever had done such a number on Sam. Then he realized what Sam had said: hypocritical.

Wasn't that interesting? Had his ex-wife found out and used it against him? Had he known when he married her or was this a recent realization? Did anyone else know?

Sam's breathing steadied after a moment, and he sat back up.

"Feel better?" Jeremy asked.

Sam nodded, although in the fading light of night and the impending storm, Jeremy thought he still looked a bit like a fish out of water.

"Your ex did a number on you, didn't she?"

"What?" Sam said.

"Your ex," Jeremy repeated. "What did she say to you to make you so tentative about everything?"

"Nothing," Sam said immediately. "She just wanted out. She deserves someone who really loves her."

"What about someone who really loves you?" Jeremy asked. "Don't you deserve that too?"

"An out-of-work office manager with no social skills, a thickening waistline, and receding hair?" Sam countered. "Sure. They're lining up at the door."

"That's exactly what I'm talking about," Jeremy said. "That kind of statement right there. Who made you believe that?"

"The mirror," Sam replied.

Jeremy let that part go. If Sam wasn't ready to talk to him, Jeremy couldn't force his confidence. He could, however, address the content of what Sam said. "Then you need a new mirror. Because, first of all, last time I checked, you weren't out of work anymore. Unless you think Caine hired you out of pity?"

Sam took just long enough to answer that Jeremy knew he really did believe that, even if he shook his head.

Jeremy nearly snorted in disbelief. "Let me tell you something about sheep stations, at least ones the size of Taylor Peak and Lang Downs. Most years, the difference between running in the black and in the red is one or two lambs. All the worth of the station is on paper, tied up in the land and the buildings and the equipment and the livestock. Money comes in twice a year, when the lambs are sold in autumn and after the shearing in the spring, when we sell the wool. The rest of the year, it's a question of pinching pennies and hoping nothing breaks or needs to be replaced because until the next season, there's no guarantee of how much money will come in to keep things running. Pity doesn't have any place in running a station. If Caine hired you, it's because he believes doing so is in the best interest of the station. I don't know a lot about his background, but I know he got a business degree in the US. A Yank degree might not be worth a lot here, but it proves he knows his way around money, which tells me you impressed him, and that, in turn, impresses me."

"That doesn't change the rest of it," Sam said. "You can hardly argue about my hairline."

Jeremy rolled his eyes. "There's a lot more to loving someone than how thick their hair is, you know. By the time my mother died, my father had a beer belly big enough to merit its own time zone and no hair whatsoever, but she still loved him as much as the day they met. And your hairline is fine. I just thought you had a high forehead, not that you were losing your hair."

"I appreciate what you're doing," Sam said. "Really. But you don't need to. I know what I am and what I'm not. I've come to terms with it. I don't need anyone's pity."

"If that's what this was, that might sway me," Jeremy said, "but I didn't spend the day talking to you out of pity. I didn't offer to teach you about the station out of pity. I enjoyed your company today, and that's far more important than how cut you are or whether you're losing a little hair. You don't have to believe me, but I need to say it at least this once: I think you're an interesting, attractive man, and I'd like to get to know you better, but I realize you're in the middle of a divorce and that you have issues to work out around that, so I'm not going to push. I am, however, going to be your friend."

EIGHT

SAM walked into the station office the next morning, booted up the computer, and did his best to pretend he'd gotten a good night's sleep and that everything was normal. Nobody else had to know his conversation with Jeremy on the way back from Boorowa the day before had sent him into a complete tailspin.

Caine walked in a few minutes later. "You're in here early today," he said with a smile. "Things are more laid-back in the winter. Less to do in the paddocks, and all."

Sam summoned a smile, refusing to acknowledge how fake it felt. "Jeremy said something to that effect yesterday, but we hadn't talked about it, and I didn't want to presume."

"Now we've talked about it," Caine said. "Macklin was talking about riding out to check on some of the drover's huts in a little bit, to make sure they weathered last night's storm and that they're sound when the next one comes."

"Is storm damage a problem?" Sam asked.

"It can be," Caine replied. "We usually get one or two bad storms a winter, but Macklin assures me that's completely unpredictable."

"Your insurance should cover those repairs," Sam said.

"It might," Caine agreed, "but the cost of replacing a few shingles isn't worth the hassle of having the insurance inspector come out."

"You should look into it, though," Sam said. "If you use a digital camera with a timestamp, you have proof of when the picture was taken. There's no reason to pay for repairs that should be covered. You spend enough in maintenance without adding to it. Even if you do the repairs yourself, you could submit a claim for reimbursement."

"Won't submitting too many claims drive up our premiums?" Caine asked. "I'd rather keep the premiums relatively low and absorb small costs here and there than have them go up because we're nickel-and-diming them to death."

"I'd have to look at the details of your coverage and the company's policy," Sam replied, "but if that's the case, I'd suggest looking for a different insurance company. What's the point in having insurance if you're afraid to submit a claim?"

"It's the same policy Uncle Michael had," Caine admitted. "There were so many other things to deal with after his death that reviewing the insurance policies wasn't even on the priority list, much less near the top."

"Do you have the policy?" Sam asked. "I took care of stuff like that at the hardware store. I'd be glad to read through it and let you know what I think."

Caine chuckled. "I'm sure I have it somewhere." He gestured to the file cabinets lining one wall of the office. "But you see what I inherited. I haven't even begun to scratch the surface. I keep saying I'll make time to go through it all, but not today."

Sam nodded. "There's no rush, I suppose. Just document any damage you find because we can deduct the cost of any repairs we don't submit to our insurance company."

"I'll take my camera with me," Caine said.

"Caine?"

"I'll be right there," Caine called back to Macklin. "Get the horses ready, and I'll meet you outside."

Macklin made a sound of acknowledgment before the sound of footsteps signaled his departure. "One other thing before I go," Caine said. "If I wanted to go about finding someone in Tumut, or who used to live in Tumut, how would I go about it?"

"Do you have a name?" Sam asked.

"Yes," Caine said. "Sarah Armstrong."

Sam raised his eyebrows. "I take it this is a secret?"

"Yes," Caine said. "If what I find is bad news, it's better if Macklin doesn't know."

"He's waiting for you," Sam said. "I'll think about what your options might be and let you know."

"Thanks, Sam, and feel free to dig through those files if you're so inclined. If not, we'll go through them together another day."

Sam waited until Caine left before eyeing the file cabinets suspiciously. He had a feeling he wasn't going to like what he found when he opened them. Caine's records from the past year and a half were meticulous, but there was a distinct lack of information for a lot of things from before that. From what everyone had said about Michael Lang since Sam's arrival, Sam was sure the information was there, just not in the most accessible form. With a sigh, he pulled open the first drawer and went to work.

He'd sorted the contents of the first drawer into three piles (too old to bother with, relevant, and to deal with immediately) when the sound of someone clearing his throat drew Sam's attention. He couldn't stop the smile that crossed his face at the sight of Jeremy standing in the doorway, hat in hand and in sock feet, even with all the uncomfortable thoughts from the previous night. "Hi."

"Hi," Jeremy said. "You look busy."

"Just sorting through stuff," Sam said. "Mr. Lang might have been a good stockman, but his organizational skills left something to be desired."

Jeremy laughed. "I told you we stockman preferred animals to numbers. I was coming to see if I could tempt you outside for your first riding lesson, but maybe I'll just stand here and watch you instead."

"I'm not doing anything interesting," Sam said with a puzzled laugh. "Watching someone else sort papers is about as exciting as watching paint dry."

"Maybe, but watching you make sense of all those papers has potential," Jeremy said with an exaggerated leer. "I told you the thought of you being all competent got me hot and bothered."

Sam flushed all the way to the roots of his hair. His receding hair. "You didn't say anything of the sort yesterday. You said I was interesting."

"Interesting *and* attractive," Jeremy said. "And I also said the fact that you could make sense out of all the business stuff when I couldn't was seriously impressive. When I said it, I didn't realize you were gay, so I left off the turn-on part. I didn't want to freak you out, but now that I know I have a chance, I'm going to mention it every time I can."

"Please don't make fun of me," Sam said, unable to hold Jeremy's gaze.

"I'm not making fun of you," Jeremy said as he came into the room and sat down on the floor next to Sam. "I wouldn't do that."

No, Sam had to admit to himself, Jeremy was a lot of things, but the schoolyard bully was not one of them. He wouldn't make fun of someone else for being smart instead of athletic. "Sorry, old habits."

"We're going to work on that," Jeremy said. "So, explain to me what you're doing and tell me how I can help."

Sam considered the piles of paper he'd already sorted through. The classifications made sense to him, but they wouldn't to Jeremy, not if he was really as clueless where business was concerned as he claimed to be. "Open the next drawer," he said. "You can start sorting things by date. Anything over ten years old in one pile. Anything three to ten years old in another pile, and anything more recent than that in a third pile. The older stuff is, the less likely I am to need to look at it immediately. Unless it looks like an insurance policy. Then I need to see it no matter how old it is."

"I can do that," Jeremy said. He opened the next drawer and got to work.

Sam expected his presence to be a distraction, with all the talk of attraction and everything, but Jeremy settled in quietly, only occasionally interrupting Sam's sorting to ask a question or make an observation. It turned out to be a far more peaceful morning than he could have anticipated.

The sound of his stomach growling drew both their attention to the clock.

"Look at that," Jeremy said. "Lunchtime already. Can we take a break, boss, or are you going to make me work through lunch with nothing to fill my poor empty belly?"

Sam laughed at that, since it was his own empty belly making noise. "Let's go. We've gotten more done than I could have by myself. We've earned a break."

Jeremy bounced to his feet with the ease of a man in full control of his body. Sam envied the grace of his movements, but didn't try to imitate them. He'd make a fool of himself if he did. He braced his arm on the nearby chair when Jeremy reached down and offered his hand. Sam took it and let Jeremy pull him to his feet, ignoring the shiver of desire at how big Jeremy's hand felt in his and how easily Jeremy did it. He was wearing long sleeves again today, but Sam had gotten a glimpse of the arms underneath the shirt yesterday. He'd never known he had an arm fetish until now, but that glimpse of skin had done things to his insides.

The canteen was pretty much deserted when they walked in, not that Sam had expected otherwise. Even at the height of summer, most of the jackaroos took sandwiches with them for lunch rather than returning to the canteen. With all but the year-rounders gone now, that seemed to hold even more true. A plate of sandwiches sat on the counter under plastic wrap, so Sam and Jeremy grabbed plates and helped themselves. "So what's on the agenda for this afternoon?"

"I'd planned on working in the office all day," Sam said, "but if you have something else you need to do, I understand. I can work by myself. It's not a problem."

"That's not what I said or what I meant," Jeremy said. "You mentioned moving into the bunkhouse. I thought I'd give you a hand with your things if you wanted, and I promised to show you how a station runs."

"I probably ought to check with Caine before I move into the bunkhouse," Sam said. "I mean, I know the rooms are empty, but there's a difference between staying in Neil's spare room and living in the bunkhouse."

"Really?"

"Yes, really," Sam said. "If I'm in Neil's spare room, I'm dependent on his generosity. In the bunkhouse, I'm dependent on Caine's generosity."

"How do you figure that?" Jeremy asked. "Unless things are a whole lot different here, Caine owns Neil's house too. Neil gets to use it as part of his employment package, but it's still station property. If he decided to leave, he wouldn't get any value from the house, just whatever belongings of his he'd moved into it."

"Oh," Sam said. "I guess I hadn't thought about it that way."

"That's what you get for taking up with the son of a grazier," Jeremy said with a grin. "I might not have a head for business, but I picked up a few details here and there over the years."

"So you're saying I should stick with you?" Sam asked, feeling daring for flirting with Jeremy.

"Definitely," Jeremy replied, his grin widening. "I won't steer you wrong."

"I'd still feel better if we asked Caine before I moved," Sam said. "Even if it makes no functional difference, it feels different to me."

"Did he say where he was going to be today?" Jeremy asked.

"He said something about checking the drover's huts for storm damage," Sam replied.

"Uh-huh," Jeremy joked. "Let me guess. Macklin went with him."

"What's wrong with that?"

"Nothing's wrong with it," Jeremy replied. "It's a very responsible thing for them to do after a storm like the one last night. It speaks well of their concern for their property and their employees."

"Then why are you snickering?"

"Because the drover's huts are probably the only place on the station besides their bedroom where they'd have any privacy," Jeremy said. "I'm sure it's just coincidental that Macklin decided to go with Caine today."

Sam felt himself flush again, something he seemed to do with alarming regularity around Jeremy. "You don't really think they rode out today just for that, do you?"

"No," Jeremy replied. "I'm sure they will come back with a complete list of repairs that need to be made after the storm last night. I'm just also willing to bet either one of them could do the same job faster alone than they'll do together."

"You're terrible," Sam said. "They're our bosses. We shouldn't gossip about them like that."

"There's nothing malicious in it," Jeremy assured him. "I think it's pretty awesome, actually. Two years ago, if you'd told me it could happen in my backyard, I would have laughed at the outlandishness of the thought, and now I'm talking about it like it's the most normal thing in the world."

"Lang Downs is a pretty special place."

"Lang Downs is a miracle," Jeremy amended. "A bloody miracle, and if you don't believe that, ask Chris how he ended up here. Hell, ask Macklin how he ended up here. Or Kami. Or Patrick. I'd bet most of the year-rounders have a story to tell about how this place changed their lives. I never knew what drove Michael Lang, but even as a young child, I knew things were different here when I came to visit. That's even more the case now."

"Because Caine and Macklin are together?"

"Because they're open about being together," Jeremy said. "I always wondered about Mr. Lang and his foreman, but it wasn't something anyone talked about. Caine and Macklin aren't hiding. They might not walk around holding hands or kissing or anything like that where people can see them, but you can't live on this station and have any doubts about their relationship. And that's special."

"Always?" Sam asked. "When did you start thinking about being gay?"

"When I was a teenager," Jeremy said. "The other boys on the station all wanted to sneak around the jillaroos' bunkhouse to try to catch a glimpse of the girls naked. I tagged along because it was what was expected, but I far preferred hanging out with the jackaroos. Most of them didn't think twice about walking around their bunkhouse half undressed or more. I wasn't a little kid, and I had all the same equipment they did, so what was there to worry about?"

"Shame on you," Sam scolded, but he couldn't stop the smile at the thought of an adolescent Jeremy spying on the jackaroos in plain sight. "They had no clue, did they?"

"Of course not," Jeremy said. "I was always careful to leave before I gave anything away. It sure made for some good fantasy material, though."

"Remind me not to take a shower while you're in the bunkhouse," Sam teased.

"I wouldn't do that now," Jeremy promised. "I had no sense of boundaries when I was fourteen. I have a little better sense of propriety at thirty-four. I have the courtesy to wait until I'm invited these days."

Sam flushed again, this time at the thought of someday working up the courage to invite Jeremy to join him in the showers. Maybe in a few months, when living on the station had gotten rid of some of the flab on his body. The thought of seeing Jeremy, though, had quite the appeal. They were more or less of a height, although Jeremy was maybe an inch taller, but the similarities pretty much ended there. Jeremy was built. That was the only word for it. Not like a bodybuilder, but like hard work and a lifetime in the outback. His shoulders were broad, and if the rest of his arms corresponded with the glimpse Sam had gotten of his forearms, they would be solid. The clothes Jeremy wore around the station weren't designed to show off his physique, but they fit well enough to give a hint of equally toned muscles everywhere else. Sam's imagination didn't have any trouble filling in the rest.

"Did I scare you off?" Jeremy asked.

"What? No, just remembering something," Sam said quickly. Too quickly, if the slow smile that spread over Jeremy's face was any indication.

"So what about you?" Jeremy asked. "When did you figure it out?"

"I think I probably always knew," Sam admitted, "but I only stopped pretending, even to myself, about a year ago. I married Alison to appease my father. Neil came by his homophobia honestly. I liked her, she liked me, it seemed like the best I was going to get, and it even worked for a while. Not great, but not terrible either. Then I lost my job and couldn't find another one, and she lost patience with me. Everything went to hell, and I figured I didn't have anything else to lose, so I went to a gay bar and let someone pick me up. It was a shit thing to do, but it proved what I'd always tried to deny."

Jeremy just nodded, an inscrutable look on his face.

"Well, now that I've totally killed the mood," Sam joked, trying to lighten the pall that had settled over their conversation, "I suppose I should get back to work."

"No," Jeremy said, "you should come outside with me for a couple of hours. Chris isn't using Titan today, so it's time for your first riding lesson."

"I've got work to do," Sam protested. "Those files won't sort themselves."

"No, but I helped you sort all morning," Jeremy reminded him, "and I'll help again later if you want. You need some fresh air. You'll work better later for taking a break now."

Sam wasn't sure he bought that logic, but the idea of spending a few hours outside with Jeremy, even making a fool of himself, as he was sure he would, was far more appealing than going back to sorting old records. "Okay. Let's go see what you can teach me."

NINE

JEREMY led Sam out to the paddock where the horses stayed when they weren't being ridden. "Have you ever ridden a horse before?"

Sam shook his head. "Never really had a chance. It wasn't something that came up in my line of work."

Jeremy chuckled. "No, I can see that, although some people ride for pleasure too."

"Neil was always the athletic one, not me."

Jeremy ducked between the fence posts and walked over to the bay gelding Jesse had suggested when Jeremy asked about a good horse for a beginning rider. Jeremy had ignored Jesse's smirk at the question. "Come on, Titan," he said, grabbing the horse's halter. "Come meet Sam."

Titan followed Jeremy docilely to the edge of the fence. "Say hi, Sam."

Sam held out his hand tentatively. Titan snuffled at it, lipping Sam's palm eagerly. "He wants a treat," Jeremy explained. "He's apparently a favorite with the jackaroos because everyone's always bringing him apples and carrots and things."

"You should have told me. I would have gotten something from the canteen."

"Here," Jeremy said, offering Sam the apple he'd snagged on their way out. "He'll appreciate it more than I would. Keep your hand flat. Let him take it from your palm."

Sam did as Jeremy said, put the apple in the palm of his hand, and extended it to Titan again. Titan snatched it, biting it in two with one chomp of his huge teeth.

"That's bloody scary," Sam said.

"Nah, he's not a biter. I asked," Jeremy reassured him. "He's just a glutton."

"So what now?" Sam asked.

"Now we saddle up and let you get used to seeing the world from a different angle," Jeremy said. "I'll grab the tack. You stay here and get better acquainted. He'll be your mount, so you'll want to get to know him."

Jeremy left Sam with Titan while he went through the shearing sheds to the tack room. He grabbed everything he needed and went back outside in time to see Titan head-butt Sam, knocking him back several steps. Sam laughed and scratched beneath Titan's forelock. The sound hit Jeremy like a ton of bricks. It was relaxed and carefree, the happiest sound Jeremy had heard from Sam since they'd started talking. Even the few times Sam had laughed the day before hadn't been as easy. Jeremy resolved to hear more of that sound, whether by making sure Sam spent plenty of time with Titan or by learning how to elicit it himself. Sam hadn't answered him yesterday when he'd asked who had given Sam such an inferiority complex, but the man laughing with Titan now wasn't thinking about negative self-image or anything other than the sheer enjoyment of a cool fall day and a big lug of a horse who loved anyone who brought him treats. This was the man Jeremy wanted to get to know.

Now he regretted sending Arrow with Chris and Jesse that morning. He wondered if his dog would have the same effect on Sam as Titan had. If so, Jeremy wasn't letting Arrow out of Sam's sight.

"Looks like you're making friends," Jeremy said, setting the saddle down on the top rail of the fence. As soon as Sam realized he was there, Jeremy could see the walls go back up behind Sam's eyes. He cursed inwardly, but he couldn't very well teach Sam to ride from a distance.

"He's very friendly," Sam said.

"That he is," Jeremy agreed. He climbed through the fence again and grabbed a hard brush. "Give me just a minute to brush him down so he won't have anything to rub sores under the saddle and then we can tack him up and get started."

"He doesn't look dirty," Sam said.

"No, but he spends his days outside, so there's always dust and dirt on his coat. It's always better to be careful. Think about how you'd feel if you had something in your shoe and then had to walk around that way for hours."

"Yeah, that wouldn't be pleasant."

"Which is why we always brush the horses before we tack them up," Jeremy said. He finished up and grabbed a hoof pick to check Titan's shoes. When those were clean too, he took the saddle pad and laid it across Titan's back. "Hand me the saddle."

Sam lifted the heavy stock saddle off the fence rail and handed it to Jeremy. He hefted it onto Titan's back and cinched the girth. Titan let out a huff and shook his mane.

"I'm not sure he likes that," Sam said.

"Probably not," Jeremy agreed, "but he'd like it even less if the saddle wasn't secure and kept slipping around on his back." He slipped Titan's bridle over his ears and handed the reins to Sam. "Always walk on his left side with your right hand on the reins under his chin. From what everyone said, Titan's not likely to try anything or be bothered by you standing on his other side, but you might as well develop good habits now for when you move on to other horses."

"You seem pretty sure I'm going to move on to other horses," Sam observed.

"You work on a sheep station," Jeremy replied. "You'll pick up enough that you'll be riding other horses before long. It's just the nature of the situation."

"If you say so," Sam said. They led Titan to an empty paddock.

"Okay, up you go," Jeremy said, helping Sam mount. "How do the stirrups feel?"

Sam shifted around in the saddle a bit. Once he was settled, Jeremy checked the length of the stirrups and made sure his feet were positioned properly. He felt Sam start in surprise when Jeremy ran his hand up Sam's calf the first time, but Jeremy didn't let that deter him. He really did need to make sure Sam was settled correctly so he didn't fall and get hurt, but he wasn't above taking the excuse to touch Sam either.

"Okay, keep your heels down," Jeremy said. "If you were to fall, you don't want your foot to get stuck in the stirrup. That's a good way to get dragged."

"Maybe this isn't such a good idea," Sam said.

"It's a perfectly good idea," Jeremy insisted. "If you do what I tell you and pay attention to your form, you won't get hurt. It just takes practice and paying attention."

"If you're sure," Sam said.

"I'm sure," Jeremy said, patting Titan on the rump. "Tap his sides a bit with your heels to get him walking."

Sam did as Jeremy directed, and Jeremy settled back to watch Sam's reactions to the movement of the horse, to the new experience, to everything about it. He didn't bother giving more instructions at the moment. If Sam couldn't figure it out for himself, Jeremy could help him out in a few minutes. For now, though, he let Sam mess around on his own.

Without constant conversation to remind Sam that Jeremy was there, his expression relaxed again, showing some of the wonder he felt. Jeremy figured that was worth his silence, especially when Sam turned to him and grinned excitedly.

"So what do I do now?"

Jeremy explained how to use the reins to tell Titan where to go, and then he sat back again and watched. He was pretty sure he could spend hours watching Sam smile and not get bored of it.

They spent the next two hours with Sam guiding Titan around the paddock and various obstacle courses Jeremy set up so he could work on his steering skills, and with each minute that passed, Jeremy could see Sam relaxing more.

"Are you ready to go back in?" Jeremy asked eventually, hiding his delight when Sam's face fell. If Sam enjoyed riding that much, he'd be easier to persuade the next time Jeremy came to steal him away for a lesson.

"Already?"

"It's been two hours. You're going to be sore tomorrow. Riding is harder work than you realize."

"It doesn't feel like I've done any work," Sam said.

Jeremy grinned. "Get off Titan and see how your legs feel then."

Sam slid off Titan's back and didn't manage to bite back a yelp when his legs gave out beneath him. Jeremy caught his arm to steady him.

"Okay, maybe two hours was too much for my first lesson."

Jeremy laughed. "Go lean on the fence. I'll untack Titan and put everything away. Take some Nurofen tonight and soak in a hot bath. It'll help relax your muscles. You'll probably feel it for a couple of days, but it's like anything else: use the muscles and they'll get used to it."

Sam hobbled to the fence while Jeremy untacked Titan and led him back to the other paddock. As he was returning to get the tack so he could put it away, Caine and Macklin rode back in. Caine took one look at Sam and shot Jeremy a grin. "Have you been abusing my new office manager?"

"Just giving him a little riding lesson, boss," Jeremy replied with an answering grin. "I figured the more he knew about how the station worked, the better he'd be able to handle all the paperwork."

"Did you find a lot of storm damage?" Sam asked from where he continued to lean against the fence.

Jeremy wasn't as interested in Caine's answer as he was in the smile that crossed Caine's face so fast it was barely there before he replied. Yep, whatever else they'd found, they'd definitely taken advantage of the time alone.

"Hey, Caine," Jeremy said after Caine had finished detailing the storm damage, "Sam was thinking about moving out of Neil's house and into the bunkhouse to give the newlyweds some privacy now that he's not just a guest and is going to be staying on, but we thought we should check with you first."

"That shouldn't be a problem this winter," Caine said. "We'll have to look at space when we start hiring in the spring, but that gives us four months to figure things out. Do you need any help moving your things, Sam?"

"I already offered to help," Jeremy jumped in even as Sam said, "I don't have that much to move."

Caine looked amused by them, so Jeremy took that as a good sign. "Come on, Sam. Let's get the rest of the tack put away, and then we can move your stuff."

"If you need anything to spruce up the room, you're welcome to raid the guest rooms in the big house. It's not like they get a lot of use," Caine added as he and Macklin turned their horses toward the far paddock.

Jeremy grabbed the saddle and pad and handed the bridle to Sam. "I'll show you where to put everything, and next time, I'll teach you how to get Titan dressed."

Sam nodded and followed Jeremy back to the tack room, walking with the peculiar stiff bow-legged gait unique to new riders. They stowed the tack back in its spot.

"Let's go pack your stuff up,' Jeremy said.

"I really don't have much," Sam protested. "One suitcase plus the stuff I bought yesterday, and I didn't even unpack most of that."

"Then it'll be a quick move," Jeremy said, not ready to let Sam out of his sight just yet. He'd have to eventually, since he knew Sam wasn't ready for an invitation to bed, or rather, that Sam wouldn't take an invitation the right way. Jeremy could be patient. They had all winter alone together in the bunkhouse.

Sam hadn't been kidding when he said he didn't have much to move. Jeremy didn't have all that much more, given the way he'd left Taylor Peak, but something about that single suitcase being the sum total of Sam's life to date struck him as incredibly sad. "You get the bags from yesterday. I'll get the suitcase," Jeremy offered.

"I'm not some helpless girl in need of rescuing," Sam snapped. "I can carry my own bloody suitcase."

"I never said you were," Jeremy replied. "I was just trying to help."

Sam sighed. "I'm sorry. You didn't deserve that. It's just…."

"Just what?"

"My life has sucked for so long, and suddenly it seems like everything's going right. Neil didn't freak out when I told him I was gay, Caine offered me a job, complete with a roof over my head, you're flirting with me like you mean it…. It's all too good to be true, you know?"

"No," Jeremy said, "I don't know." That wasn't completely true. He'd always thought of Lang Downs as a little bit of a miracle, even more after Caine and Macklin had taken him in much as they had Sam, but Sam's problem wasn't believing in Lang Downs, it was believing he deserved anything good. "Why shouldn't you have good things? Why shouldn't I flirt with you?"

"Because you don't really mean it," Sam said, "and I'm tired of being a pity fuck or someone men use just to get their rocks off."

"I can't decide if I'm flattered you'd think I'd put this much effort into a pity fuck or if I'm insulted you'd think I'd treat anyone that way," Jeremy said after a moment. "Yes, I've been flirting with you all day. I think you're an attractive, interesting man who I'd like to get to know better. If that goes well, then maybe, and I do mean maybe, we could talk about doing more than just hanging out together, because, all joking aside, I'm not stupid enough to shit in my own backyard. If we do this, it'll be because we both want it and we're both serious about trying to make something work. I've seen what happens when relationships go sour on a station, the two people stuck in the same place, unable to ever really get away from each other unless one of them decides to quit. I'm not going to take that risk on a whim."

"You've known me for all of three days," Sam said. "How can you even think in those terms?"

"Because the only part of what I just said that's dependent on you is the fact that I'm having the conversation with you," Jeremy said. "I'm not explaining this well." He took a deep breath. "Look, let's move your stuff and get you settled, and then I promise I'll try to explain this in a way that makes sense."

Sam didn't look convinced, but he let Jeremy take the bag with his purchases from the day before. Jeremy considered it a victory that Sam let him help at all. They took everything to the bunkhouse, and Sam picked a room to use, the one farthest from Jeremy's, he couldn't help but notice sadly. He didn't protest, though. Sam had to be comfortable or everything else was moot.

Sam set his things on the bed and walked back into the common room, shutting the door behind him in a way that made it clear Jeremy wasn't welcome inside. "Okay, explain."

Jeremy grabbed a beer from his stash. "Want one?"

Sam shook his head, so Jeremy took a swig and came to sit in one of the chairs scattered around the room. "I'm thirty-four," Jeremy said. "I did the casual thing in uni, and even occasionally later, when I'd take a week or two in the winter and go to Melbourne or Sydney to burn off steam, but it was always clear upfront what my partner and I expected out of those encounters. We both got what we wanted—no harm, no foul. But I'm not twenty anymore, and I don't want the same things I did then, especially since Caine came and I started realizing I didn't have to settle for whatever I could get."

Sam didn't look convinced yet, but he was listening, so Jeremy forged ahead.

"About the same time, we had a blowup on the station. One of the jillaroos got pregnant. The bloke she had been sleeping with dropped her as fast as he could. She'd thought they were serious. He'd thought they were fucking around. The rest of the summer was miserable for everyone, with people taking sides and the two of them refusing to work together. I thought Devlin was going to blow a gasket and fire them both. By the time the season was over, everyone was exhausted from all the drama, and I'd made a promise to myself. Two promises, actually. The first was to always make sure I was clear about my possible expectations with any partner, so we didn't end up with that kind of miscommunication. The second was to only start a relationship if I saw in it the potential for something lasting."

"I can see the logic of that," Sam said slowly. "I can even see the appeal. What I can't see is how three days is enough time to make that choice."

"Because it's three days or because I'm thinking that way about you?" Jeremy asked.

"Because it's been three days," Sam said.

"So if I waited a month and said the same thing, you'd believe me?" Jeremy pressed.

"I… I don't know."

At least it was an honest answer, Jeremy thought with a sigh. "Do you want me to back off and leave you alone?"

TEN

SAM almost said yes because then he wouldn't have to deal with the doubts and desires churning through him, but that would be the easy way out, and Jeremy wasn't the only one who'd made promises to himself recently. Sam's had been to really think about what he wanted and try to accept those things about himself. "I don't know," he repeated. "At this point, exactly two people in my life know I'm gay. Well, maybe three, if Neil told Molly. The guys I fucked around with last year don't count because they don't know me. I was a body to use, nothing more. Maybe Caine and Macklin suspect, but I haven't told them either. I never thought I'd have anything other than a loveless marriage and the occasional back-alley fumble until I got here and saw what Caine and Macklin have built. I've had all of a few weeks to get used to the idea that anything more than that is even possible, much less something I could actually have. It's a lot to take in all at once."

"I can see how that would be rough," Jeremy said. "I didn't realize it had all been so fast. I didn't mean to make you feel pressured."

"You make me feel a lot of things," Sam admitted against his better judgment, "and not all of them are bad. It's just too much too fast."

"So what do you want me to do?" Jeremy asked again. "How can I make this easier for you?"

"Honestly?" Sam asked.

Jeremy nodded.

"I really just need a friend right now. Everything is so up in the air, with the divorce and the new job and what that might mean for the divorce. I don't think Alison is out to get me or to take anything from me, but I don't want to give her grounds for anything more than what I've already agreed to. If we started something and she tried to use it against me, I could lose what little I have left."

"Two bags of clothes?" Jeremy asked.

"She could demand alimony or claim emotional distress or pain and suffering or something," Sam said.

"I'm pretty sure we could make a case against her for that," Jeremy retorted. "How often did she yell at you for not having a job?"

Sam flushed. "I couldn't even begin to count."

"And I bet that's not the only thing she said," Jeremy added.

Sam didn't answer, but memories of Alison's sharply barbed comments about everything from his appearance to his prowess—or lack thereof—in bed flooded his memory. "She was under a lot of stress.

"That's not an excuse for emotional abuse," Jeremy said. "So, we're not going to do anything to give her grounds for demanding more than she's already taken from you. How long until the divorce is final?"

"About six months. We can't actually file until we've been separated for a year, which is three months from now, and then it usually takes about three months for everything to be finalized."

"Then for the next six months, we're going to hang out as friends, get to know each other, work on your self-esteem a bit. I might flirt a little because I can't seem to help it, but I won't try anything more than that, not even a kiss," Jeremy said. "When the divorce is final and you don't have to worry about her anymore, we'll see how we both feel. Maybe you'll be right, and as I get to know you, I'll decide we're better off as friends. Maybe I'll be right, and as I get to know you, I'll just find you even more interesting and more attractive than I already do. Whichever happens, it'll be fine because we both agreed to the friendship and the later conversation.

And by that time, you won't be able to say I don't know you well enough if I'm right."

Sam swallowed hard, considering the options Jeremy had laid out. He needed a friend. There was no doubt about that. He thought, with time, he and Caine could be friends, but Caine was also his boss, and Sam wasn't sure he'd ever be able to confide in Caine completely with that barrier between them. He and Neil were closer than they'd ever been now that Sam's secret was out in the open, but Neil was so wrapped up in Molly, as he should be, that Sam wasn't sure how much time he'd have for him. Not to mention Neil had been very clear on the kinds of things he didn't want to hear. Jeremy could be that friend. He could guide Sam through life on the station. He had already proved he could listen without judging and that he'd defend Sam, even against his own screwed-up ideas.

The problem wasn't being friends with Jeremy. The problem was Jeremy's insistence that they revisit the idea of something more, because as long as that was on the table as an eventual option between them, Sam wouldn't be able to stop himself from dreaming. He'd have to be stupid not to want everything he could get from a man like Jeremy, whether that was one night of pleasure or a lifetime of companionship. He just couldn't believe a man like Jeremy would want any of that from him.

Jeremy would probably say that was Alison talking. He was probably even right, but that didn't make it any easier to dismiss the doubts when he'd never been the dashing type, even before he started losing his hair. He'd never been the one with the buff body all the girls drooled over. He was barely one step up from the nerds they'd made fun of. Only the lack of glasses had saved him from that. He was good at what he did, but it wasn't glamorous or dashing or anything special. He was an office drone, even if he had moved up to managing the office. He hadn't turned his abilities with numbers into a fat stock portfolio or leveraged it to start his own business. He'd been content to run the hardware store for the Smiths, never thinking they might close it when they retired instead of selling it to someone who would be glad to have an office manager who already knew his way around the books.

He'd been genuinely stunned when Alison had agreed to marry him, and that had been ten years and twenty pounds ago. If he got as much exercise on the station as he had today, he might lose the twenty pounds, but nothing could give him back the ten years.

Jeremy was only about a year younger than him, but he could have been anywhere between twenty-five and forty. The lines on his face from the sun and wind proclaimed he wasn't a kid anymore, but they made him look strong, not old. He would probably look exactly the same in another ten years. Sam couldn't say the same about himself.

That was the part of all of this Sam couldn't wrap his mind around. With his looks, his sense of fun, and that devilish grin, Jeremy could have anyone he wanted, male or female. The guys in the bars Sam had gone to when he needed to forget about everything for a while would be all over someone like Jeremy, and they wouldn't just want him for the night. They'd want to snatch him up and keep him. So why would someone like that, someone who could have his choice of lovers, want someone like Sam?

They could be friends. Sam would love to have a friend like Jeremy, but if Jeremy kept putting the possibility of more on the table, Sam would end up wanting it. Oh, who was he kidding? He already wanted it. He just didn't understand it and so couldn't believe in it. To have it within reach and lose it would be the worst kind of torture.

"Sam?"

"Sorry, just thinking."

"Let me guess," Jeremy said. "You were wondering what I could possibly see in you and trying to figure out how to make it hurt less when I change my mind."

Sam flushed. "How do you do that?"

"It's not that hard," Jeremy said. "I already know you don't think of yourself as being attractive. You've already asked me how I could possibly find you interesting. Which means one of two things: either you're trying to figure out how to let me down gently, or you're trying to talk yourself out of going along with my plan."

He leaned in so close Sam could practically feel his breath. He ached to lean forward and see what it would feel like to kiss him, but he didn't close the distance between them.

"If you're trying to let me down gently, don't," Jeremy said. "If you really aren't interested in anything more than friendship, just say so. I'm a big boy. I can handle it. If you're trying to talk yourself out of it, stop. Nothing's going to happen until your divorce is final, so there's nothing to talk yourself out of."

"I wasn't trying to let you down gently," Sam admitted.

Jeremy flashed that grin again, the one that made Sam's stomach flip. "Good. Everything else can wait."

Sam still wasn't convinced, but arguing with Jeremy was like trying to hold on to smoke. He'd just have to guard his heart so that when the six months were up and Jeremy changed his mind, it wouldn't hurt too much.

"Jeremy?"

Jeremy straightened up. "Yes, I'm here," he called back.

Chris and Jesse came in a moment later, wiped their feet on the mat by the doorway, and pulled off their boots. A beautiful brown kelpie with bright blue eyes came bounding in after them, right up to Jeremy.

"Hi, Arrow," Jeremy said, scratching the dog's ears. "Did you have a good day?"

"He was a lot of help," Jesse said. "Thanks for letting us borrow him."

"You're welcome," Jeremy replied. "Sam, have you met Arrow yet?"

"No," Sam said, holding out his hand to the dog.

"Go on, boy," Jeremy said. "Go say hi to Sam."

The dog padded across the room and sniffed at Sam's hand before plopping down at his feet and leaning his muzzle against Sam's leg. Sam smiled as he scratched behind Arrow's ears the way he'd seen Jeremy do. "He's beautiful."

"I've had him since he was a pup," Jeremy said. "I trained him myself."

"And very well," Jesse added.

"You want a beer?" Jeremy asked. "I owe you after what I drank at your place the other night."

"I wouldn't say no," Jesse replied. "If we aren't intruding."

"Not at all," Jeremy said. "Sam decided the bunkhouse was better than his brother's guest room, so we're just getting him settled in here. Nothing to intrude on. You sure you don't want anything, Sam?"

"Fine, I'll take one," Sam said, relaxing now that Chris and Jesse were there. Jeremy wouldn't push when other people were around, and Sam wouldn't mind making a few more friends. If this was going to be home now, he needed to get to know as many of the year-rounders as possible.

Jeremy passed around the beers and then settled back in his chair. Chris and Jesse took one of the couches and started describing their day. Sam sat back and just listened. He didn't really know any of the people or much about the jobs they had been sent out to do, but that didn't matter. The easy camaraderie of sitting around at the end of a long day was more than enough for him. He'd learn. He'd meet the rest of the year-rounders, and Jeremy would teach him about the kinds of jobs the jackaroos did, and eventually he'd be able to join in instead of just listening.

"So what did you do today?" Chris asked Jeremy when he and Jesse were done with their tale.

"I taught Sam to ride," Jeremy said.

"Impressive if you taught him in just one day," Jesse replied.

"He taught me how to get on and off without breaking my neck and how to guide Titan around the paddock," Sam corrected. "I wouldn't want to go anywhere without a fence just yet."

"On Titan, you'd be fine," Chris assured him. "A few months ago, I'd never been on a horse either. I won't claim to be an expert yet, but I ride well enough that they let me out of the valley now on a horse other than Titan."

"He gets stuck with all the blow-ins?" Sam asked.

"I don't know about all of them," Chris said, "but I know Caine rode him when he first got here, and then I did, and now you are. He's steady and reliable and not prone to antics. It makes him good for those of us who need a little extra patience."

"And then there's Ned," Jesse said with a laugh. "Biggest son of a bitch on the station. The only person I've ever seen ride him is Macklin. When Macklin's on his back, he's as docile as Titan. When anyone else gets near him, he turns into a bloody wild brumby."

"I'd better leave him to Macklin, then," Sam said. "I could barely handle Titan. I don't want to think about a horse only Macklin can handle."

"I'd like to try riding him sometime," Jeremy said. "If Macklin agrees, of course. I understand that he's Macklin's horse, but what good is he if no one else can ride him? I mean, Arrow's my dog, and I like to think he works best for me, but he'll go out with someone else if I send him."

"I don't know," Jesse said. "I'm just telling you what I've seen. The year-rounders don't try, and the new guys who did over the summer all ended up on their arses on the ground, even the ones who actually had some experience. I didn't try. I'm not a glutton for punishment."

"What did Macklin say about that?"

"He said if they were fool enough to try after being warned, it was their own damn fault for being idiots," Jesse said. "He never tells anyone they aren't allowed to ride Ned. He just warns them Ned doesn't like anyone but him."

The bell outside the canteen tolled, calling everyone to dinner. They tramped across the road to eat. The canteen seemed huge with fewer than half the number of bodies filling it as the day before. Sam filled his plate and joined Jeremy, Chris, and Jesse at one of the tables. A few minutes later, another group of men came in. Sam couldn't help but notice they sat as far away from Jeremy as possible.

"Do they really hate you that much?"

"They don't know me," Jeremy said. "They hate Devlin, not that I really blame them, and they assume because he's my brother, I must have been part of his schemes. They're not hurting me. I've already made friends, and Macklin and Caine trust me enough to have me here. The rest is just icing on the cake."

"It's not right," Sam insisted.

"No, it isn't," Jesse agreed, "but it's not something we can fix just like that. It's a matter of time and trust and them figuring out that Jeremy being here isn't going to change anything."

Seth and Jason came running into the canteen. "Chris, Jesse," Seth called, "Patrick says we should come over to his place after dinner. Carley made dessert."

"Are Sam and Jeremy included?" Chris asked.

"I don't know," Seth said. "Patrick didn't say."

"Yes, they're included," Jason piped up. "Dad always says it's rude to invite some people and not others, so yes, they're included."

"Then we'd love to have some of Carley's dessert," Chris said.

"Cool," Seth said. "Come on, Jase. Let's get some dinner."

"That's how attitudes change," Jeremy said with a smile. "One person at a time making a difference."

ELEVEN

SAM spent the next day alone in the office. He'd seen Jeremy at breakfast, all kitted up in his Driza-Bone. He'd apologized for not being able to spend the day with Sam again, but Macklin needed him and Arrow. Sam had been disappointed, but what could he say? Jeremy had been hired to work the station, and Sam's job was the books. The good news was that he'd finally found the station's insurance policy. The bad news was how out of date it was. Caine wasn't around to talk about it, though, so Sam set it aside for the next time Caine was free and went back to sorting papers.

The canteen was empty at lunch, even the kids on the station choosing to eat somewhere else, so Sam decided to take his sandwich back to the office with him. It was far too depressing to sit alone in the canteen.

"Where do you think you're going?"

The booming voice startled Sam so much he nearly dropped his coffee. "I was going to take my lunch back to the office."

The big aborigine humphed at that. "Come in here where it's warm. Everyone deserves a break."

Sam followed the other man obediently into the kitchen. It was considerably warmer there than in the canteen, and it smelled wonderful. "What's for dinner? It smells fantastic."

"Shepherd's pie," Kami said, "and no jokes about how appropriate that is. I've heard them all, and they're still not funny."

"I wouldn't dream of it," Sam promised. "I love shepherd's pie. My mum used to make it on cold days when we were kids."

"It sticks to your ribs and warms you up when it's cold outside," Kami agreed. "You look like you could use a little feeding up."

Sam ran his hand self-consciously over his stomach. "This doesn't need any help, thanks."

Kami looked at him critically. "Somebody's been lying to you, boyo, if they told you that. Your face is thin and your skin looks pinched. I've seen men look like that before, and it's always because they aren't eating right. You'll get plenty of exercise around here. You eat proper, or you're going to make yourself sick."

"Not much exercise in sitting in an office all day," Sam retorted.

"Maybe not, but you won't stay in there forever. Caine will want to show you something, or Macklin will ask for an opinion on a project, and the next thing you know, you'll be out there working right beside them, and that's if your brother doesn't drag you out first."

"Why would they want to do that?" Sam asked.

"Because they can't imagine anyone not loving this place as much as they do," Kami replied. "And since they're right about that far more than they're wrong, they keep doing it."

Sam couldn't begin to imagine what input he could realistically give on anything that didn't involve finances, but Kami seemed pretty convinced. "Jeremy did start teaching me to ride yesterday. Of course he ended up having to do something else today."

"Ah, so that's the way the wind blows, is it?" Kami asked. "Don't let your brother's opinion sour you on that boy. I've known him and his family since before he was born. He's the best thing to ever come out of that station, unlike his nitwit brother."

"I know Neil has his blind spots," Sam said. "I do my best not to share them."

"That's good to hear," Kami said. "I wasn't sure he was going to make it when he found out about Caine and Macklin. Does he know about you and Jeremy?"

"There isn't any 'me and Jeremy'," Sam insisted, flushing despite himself. "He's been kind to me the past couple of days while Neil's been off the station. That's all."

"Then why are you the color of one of my Thai peppers?" Kami demanded. "People don't flush like that for no reason."

"He was kind to me," Sam insisted.

"And it's been some time since anyone has been, is that it?" Kami asked. "You have the look about you."

"Why does everyone keep saying that?" Sam asked. "Just because I'm not oozing confidence out of every pore doesn't make me abused or neglected or whatever everyone seems to think I am."

"No, it doesn't," Kami agreed, "but I know a thing or two about it, having lived through it myself. I recognize the signs when I see them, and I see them all over you, in every self-deprecating comment and every defensive gesture. You're safe here, Sam. No one is going to raise a hand or a voice to you. No one is going to tear you down for being who you are. I know you have no reason to trust it yet, but Lang Downs is a safe place. Michael Lang started taking in strays from the moment he founded this station seventy years ago. Macklin, your brother, me... we're the latest in a long line of people who came here to lick our wounds and realized this was the Promised Land. Caine's carried on his uncle's tradition. Ask Chris if you don't believe me. You and Jeremy are the newest, but you aren't the first, and you won't be the last. Not while Caine and Macklin run this station. So you can accept that now or you can keep fighting it and delay being happy that much longer."

"That's the first time I've ever heard you say Uncle Michael's name," Caine said as he walked into the kitchen. "No, I wasn't eavesdropping. I figured I'd refill my coffee before I rode back out to where I left Macklin."

"When you got here, he hadn't been gone a year yet," Kami explained, "and it's considered disrespectful to speak the names of the dead before a year has passed. More than a year has passed. Go on, get out of here. Sam and I were talking."

Caine smiled at Sam. "Now you know who really runs things around here. We all live in fear of Kami."

"I can see why," Sam ventured, Caine's smile and Kami's candor giving him courage.

"I'll let you get back to your conversation," Caine said. "Oh, any thoughts on that project we were discussing, Sam?"

"A couple," Sam said, "and I found the insurance policy, which we should discuss too, when you have time."

"I'll tell Macklin I need to stay here in the office tomorrow," Caine said. "We can talk then."

"Thanks," Sam said as Caine left.

"Blow-in," Kami said with an affectionate shake of his head as he watched Caine head back outside. "He doesn't act like it now, but he was as clueless as you are when he first got here, probably even a little more so because he's a Yank. Don't ever forget that when you start thinking you can't fit in here. A little over twelve months ago, Caine arrived for the first time. Chris has only been here for about six months. It's not how long you've been here. It's how deeply you invest your heart in this place that matters."

"So you're saying if I stick around and give it a chance, I'll fit in as well as Caine does?" Sam asked.

"You'll find your own place to fit in," Kami amended. "You just have to take what's being offered."

Sam thought of Jeremy's offer from the day before, to be his friend until his divorce was finalized and then to perhaps be so much more. He couldn't let himself hope, not so soon, but it wouldn't be such a terrible thing to have a friend. It had been so long since he'd had someone for himself, not someone who was married to one of Alison's friends and so was his "friend" by default, but someone who'd chosen to be his friend. "I better get back to work. I don't want to be stuck in the office after dinner. I have things to do."

Kami smiled. "Get out of here. You're in my way anyway."

Sam flinched before the affection in Kami's tone penetrated his shock. Kami had spoken to Caine in exactly the same tone of voice. He smiled all the way back to the office, warmed by the fact that he'd apparently made another friend without even realizing it.

SAM joined Jeremy, Chris, and Jesse at dinner again. He'd expected Neil and Molly to be back already, but he didn't see them in the canteen, so either they'd been delayed or they were eating in their own house. Sam had seen a kitchen there, even if he hadn't seen either of them use it beyond preparing a cup of tea or storing bottles of beer.

"What's got you all in a twist?" Jesse asked when Sam looked around the canteen for the fifth time.

"I'm just surprised Neil and Molly aren't back yet," Sam said. "He said they'd be back today. I can't decide if I should worry or not."

"It feels later than it is," Jeremy reminded him. "It's getting dark earlier with winter approaching. I wouldn't worry yet."

"Neil knows his way around the station," Jesse assured him. "He won't get lost, and he'll know if he's in over his head. If he is, he'll find a drover's hut and stay the night. He might take risks by himself, but he's not going to risk a single hair on Molly's pretty dark head."

"That's true," Sam said. "He has a phone. He'd call if he got delayed."

"I'm sure he would," Jesse said. "You could see if Caine's heard from him. He might call the boss first."

"He'd have to," Sam said. "I don't have a phone. I couldn't afford one when I didn't have a job, and I don't really need one working in the office out here."

Jeremy frowned. "If you leave the valley, make sure you either take a radio or are with someone who has a phone. As careful as we all are, things happen, and you don't ever want to be out there without a way of communicating back if there's a problem."

"Is it really that dangerous?"

"It can be," Jeremy said. "It can also be so breathtakingly beautiful you can hardly believe it's real."

The sound of a car door slamming interrupted them. "I bet that's Neil and Molly right now," Jesse said. "You want to go check on them?"

"No, there's no need," Sam said, tensing despite himself in anticipation of Neil's reaction when he saw who Sam was sitting with. "They'll come in for dinner. I'll see them then."

Jeremy must have felt his tension because he leaned toward Sam and asked, "Do you want me to sit somewhere else?"

"No!" Sam exclaimed, though he kept his voice low. "You've been kind to me. I'm not ashamed to be your friend. I'm just not looking forward to Neil's reaction."

"I don't want to make problems for you," Jeremy said.

"Neil's the one with the problem if he can't see that you aren't your brother," Sam insisted. "I just know what he's like when it comes to making him admit he's the one with the problem."

Neil strode into the canteen with that same confident air Sam had noticed in the other year-rounders, although perhaps less in Chris and Jesse. Some of the others called out greetings that Neil answered absently as he looked around. When his gaze settled on Sam, and Neil realized who else was with him, his expression tightened, and he stalked toward their table.

Sam sighed. He'd hoped to avoid this in public, but Neil didn't seem to care about the spectacle he was making of himself, and Molly wasn't there yet to stop him.

"What are you doing?" Neil asked Sam.

"Having dinner," Sam replied, reminding himself he wasn't dependent on Neil's generosity anymore. He had a place here independent of his brother. "That is what typically happens in a canteen at this hour of the day, isn't it?"

"Don't be a drongo," Neil said. "That's not what I meant. Why are you eating dinner with *him*?"

"I'm eating dinner with my friends," Sam said, "because they invited me to join them, and I saw no reason to say no."

Neil looked like he'd eaten something unpleasant, but before he could say anything else, Molly walked up to his side and put a hand on his arm. "Neil, leave Sam alone. He's an adult and can sit wherever he wants. We'll see him at the house after dinner."

Sam hadn't planned on that exactly, but he didn't figure he could avoid it. "Yes, I'll come by after dinner, and we can talk. You told Macklin you wouldn't start anything, so don't, okay?"

Neil opened his mouth to say something, probably something biting, but Molly tugged his arm sharply, and he closed his mouth, letting her lead him away.

"Bloody hell," Sam muttered. "He's my brother and I love him, but it's a good thing he's got Molly to keep him in check, or someone would have killed him a long time ago. I'm sorry, Jeremy."

"No worries, mate," Jeremy said with a smile that even felt genuine. "I'm asking people not to judge me for my brother's actions. I owe you the same consideration."

"I suppose that's true. I'll have to pass on the beer tonight, though. I have a feeling my conversation with Neil isn't going to be short, especially once he realizes I've moved out," Sam said.

"Oh, you haven't told him?" Jesse asked gleefully. "Can I come listen to him explode?"

"Jesse," Chris said. "Be nice."

"I have a lot of respect for Neil as a stockman," Jesse said. "And I have a lot of respect for him for standing up for Caine. I really do. But he can be a little overbearing. Maybe he doesn't mean anything by it, but I can't help but want to see him taken down a peg."

"It's still private," Chris said. "I don't want anyone outside our family to hear when I have to talk to Seth about stuff. Sam shouldn't have to have an audience for his family disputes either."

"Fine," Jesse said, "but I want to know how it goes."

"It's going to go like this," Sam said. "I'm going to remind him that I'm his *older* brother and that I'm perfectly capable of making decisions for myself. I'm going to tell him that I appreciate him letting me stay with him and Molly when I first got here, but that I need space of my own and so do they. And then I'm going to ask them about their wedding plans. Neil will probably bluster and protest, but I'm almost thirty-six. He can't order me around. It doesn't work that way."

"We can have our beer in the bunkhouse tonight," Jeremy broke in. "That way you can make sure Sam comes home okay."

"You make it sound like I'm Seth's age," Sam protested.

"It's not about how old you are," Jeremy said. "It's about how hard it is to argue with your brother, no matter your age. Believe me, I know."

Sam couldn't dispute that. He'd been there the last time Jeremy argued with his brother, and it hadn't been pretty. "Fine, but I'm telling you, it won't be like that."

Chris changed the subject then, asking Jesse about the repairs they'd be doing on the station equipment over the winter. Sam knew nothing about engines, but Jesse obviously did as he chatted happily about tractors and more.

Sam lingered as long as he could over the meal, but eventually he couldn't put it off any longer. "I'll talk to you later, mates," he said as he rose to deposit his plate with the dirty dishes.

Neil lay in wait for him just inside the door to his house. "You know what I think of Taylor," he said the minute Sam stepped inside.

"I do," Sam said. "I also know what Caine and Macklin think of him, and at the moment, I'm more inclined to trust their judgment than yours."

"I'm your brother!"

"You are," Sam agreed, "but they're the bosses around here, and they're the ones who made the decision to hire their rival's younger brother. They're the ones with the most to lose, but they don't seem concerned about having him here. I don't see why I should give your opinion more weight than theirs, especially when Jeremy has gone out of his way to be friendly and helpful to me."

"He's using you," Neil warned.

"Why would you even think something like that?" Sam demanded. "Seriously, Neil, are you even listening to yourself? If Jeremy were here with some ulterior motive or secret plan—and I think that's the most ridiculous thing I've heard since I got here— I'm the last person he'd want to get close to because I'm even newer here than he is. Besides, when we were coming back from getting supplies in Boorowa, we ran into Devlin Taylor, and he and Jeremy argued again. Taylor doesn't want Jeremy around, for whatever reason. Jeremy didn't make that up. I saw it for myself."

Neil didn't look convinced, but Sam didn't let that stop him. "Look, Neil," he said a little more calmly. "I'm not asking you to like Jeremy. I'm not asking you to work with him. But I like him, and I'd like to keep learning from him, so I am asking you to accept that. Besides, he's the only other person living in the bunkhouse at the moment, so it's not like I can avoid him."

"Wait, *other* person living in the bunkhouse? Why would you move into the bunkhouse?"

"Because I can only impose on you and Molly for so long," Sam said. "I get room and board as part of my contract with the station, so I might as well take advantage of that."

"Living here counts as room on the station," Neil said.

"Maybe, but it also means depending on you for something when I don't need to. I know it seems like I'm splitting hairs, but I spent the last nine months completely dependent on Alison's generosity, if you can call it that. I finally have the means and the opportunity to not be dependent on anyone for anything, and that feels good. Please don't ask me to give that up."

"I...."

"Just say yes," Molly said from the doorway behind them. "It isn't your choice to make for him, Neil."

"Fine," Neil said. "I need a beer. You want one?"

"Sure," Sam said, taking the peace offering for what it was.

Neil disappeared into the kitchen, and Molly came over to Sam. "Have a seat. I don't have to tell you how stubborn your brother is."

"No, you don't," Sam said. "He's always been that way."

"It has its benefits," she said, "but I know it doesn't seem that way today. He'll come around, though. He loves you, and he worries about you. You're gaunt and you look tired, even after almost four weeks here. He wouldn't argue with you this way if he didn't care about you."

"I just hate it that the person who's been the friendliest to me is the person he can't see the worth of," Sam said.

"There are years of bad blood to overcome," Molly reminded him. "I know most of it was Devlin, not Jeremy, but Neil doesn't see it that way, and you know why he doesn't?"

"Why not?"

"Because he can't imagine a world in which he would side with someone else over you," Molly said. "He can't wrap his head around Jeremy and Devlin having such a complete falling out that Jeremy would actually come here intending to stay. He can imagine them arguing, but not permanently. And if it's not permanent, then Jeremy is, in Neil's mind, just seeing things, learning things, to take back to Taylor Peak with him when he leaves, things that could perhaps be used to hurt this station."

"His loyalty has always been his best quality," Sam agreed.

"It is," Molly said. "It saved his job here after Caine saved his life. It helped save the station this summer when so many of the new jackaroos didn't know what they were doing. Nobody worked harder than Neil to make sure everything was done, not even Macklin. Of course that could be because Neil worked hard so Macklin wouldn't have to, but the end result was the same. He thinks Alison must be an idiot because she left you. The list goes on. And so he can't begin to understand how Jeremy could put anything above his brother."

"I think it was more a case of Devlin putting something above Jeremy," Sam said. "From what I could see, anyway."

"Loyalty has to go both ways," Molly said, "but the fact remains that Jeremy is here instead of on Taylor Peak with his brother, and for Neil, that can't bode well for us. He'll come around. He's loyal, not blind. He'll see that Jeremy means no harm. It'll just take time."

"I guess I just ignore him in the meantime?"

"I didn't say that," Molly said. "You should do exactly what you did tonight and call him on his shit. He trusts you. Once he gets over the shock, he'll realize that if you like and trust Jeremy, maybe he can too."

TWELVE

"YOU sure you want a tour of the sheds?" Jeremy asked as they walked down the station road later in the week. Sam had spent most of the day in the office, going over the insurance policy with Caine and helping him search for Macklin's mother. When Caine had called it a day a little early, Sam had jumped at the chance to spend an hour outdoors before dinner.

"Yes, I'm sure. I need to understand how things work, remember?"

"Don't complain about the stench, then," Jeremy said.

Sam just smiled.

The sheds did stink, but Sam found he didn't care. Jeremy explained the purpose of the different pens inside the sheds, showing him where the lambs would be kept when they were born, explaining what all the equipment was for. They'd almost reached the far end when Sam heard a pitiful mewling.

"I thought all the sheep were outside," Sam said, looking around to see where the noise was coming from.

"They are," Jeremy said, "or they're supposed to be."

"Something's in here and it's crying," Sam said. "Didn't you hear that?"

They searched in the direction of the sound until they found a tiny calico kitten trapped between the gate and the fencepost of one of the lambing pens. "Easy there, baby," Sam said, stroking the kitten's head as Jeremy released the latch on the gate. The kitten fell forward into Sam's hands, the mewling cries turning into a rumbling purr far too loud for the tiny body.

"He likes you," Jeremy said.

"He's just glad to be free of the trap he found himself in," Sam said, setting the kitten down on the ground. It immediately started crying again.

"No, he likes you," Jeremy insisted.

Sam took a step back to see what happened and the kitten followed him with a pronounced limp. "He's hurt," Sam said, scooping the kitten back up.

"Let me see him," Jeremy said.

Sam handed the kitten over gently. He watched nervously while Jeremy prodded at the tiny body. When Jeremy's fingers ran over the kitten's side, it hissed in protest. "Looks like she might have hurt her ribs while she was stuck in there."

"She?"

"Definitely a she," Jeremy said, tipping her body so Sam could see her stomach. Sam had no idea what he was supposed to be looking at. He didn't know anything about cat anatomy, but he accepted Jeremy's assertion.

"So what do we do?"

"She's a barn cat," Jeremy said. "She'll be fine in a day or two."

He started to set the kitten down, but Sam grabbed her. "You can't just leave her to fend for herself. She needs someone to take care of her. She's just a baby."

"Her mum's around here somewhere," Jeremy said. "She really will be fine. But if you want to spoil her for a few days, that's your business. Just don't come running to me when she makes a mess on your clothes or decides to use your boots as a scratching post."

"People keep cats all the time," Sam said. "How hard can it be?"

"I wouldn't know," Jeremy said. "I've always had dogs."

"A kitten can't be that different from a puppy in terms of what she needs," Sam insisted. "Food, water, somewhere to do her business, something to scratch on, maybe something to chew on...."

"If you spoil her, she's never going to learn to hunt for herself," Jeremy said. "You'll be stuck with her."

"It's just until she's not hurt anymore."

Jeremy rolled his eyes, but Sam wasn't deterred. He cradled her against his chest as they left the sheds and headed back toward the bunkhouse. "What are you going to eat?" he asked her.

"Meat," Jeremy said. "She's a hunter, or she will be if you let her learn how."

"Maybe Kami would give me the scraps from whatever he's making for dinner," Sam said. "I'd probably have to cut them up into pieces for her."

"She has claws and teeth. She can tear into the scraps just like she would a mouse or anything else she caught," Jeremy reminded him.

"Yes, but she's hurt. She's not going to feel like doing that right now," Sam insisted.

Jeremy rolled his eyes again. "Just give in right now and admit that you've got yourself a cat. You're never going to send her back to the sheds. I can tell already."

"Is that really such a terrible thing?" Sam asked.

"No," Jeremy replied, his voice softening. "It's not a terrible thing. Just watch her around Arrow until we see how they're going to get along. He's a lot bigger than she is, and he's not hurt."

"I guess she needs a name, then," Sam said.

"Eventually," Jeremy agreed, "but you can wait a day or two to see if something strikes you."

"Where did Arrow's name come from?" Sam asked.

"It was a joke, actually," Jeremy said. "He was one of a litter of seven. The other six were typical puppies, tumbling over each other, zigzagging around, but Arrow was always different. He'd pick a target and go straight to it, no zigzagging, no tumbling and playing around, just straight as an arrow to his goal."

"That's a great story," Sam said.

"Yeah, the name just stuck after that. I'm sure his brothers and sisters grew out of that puppy phase and are now fantastic sheep dogs too, but Arrow was definitely a step ahead of them back then."

"Do you think he'll mind having a cat around?" Sam asked.

"Most of the time when I've seen cats and dogs have trouble living together, it's because the cat was already afraid of dogs when the dog arrived," Jeremy said. "Dogs usually adapt better since the cat isn't really a threat. He'll probably just see her as something else to herd around and take care of. And she's young enough to get past being scared of him."

"Sam, Jeremy, what you got there?" Jason asked, running over to them.

"Sam found a kitten stuck in the sheds," Jeremy said. "He thinks she can't take care of herself and needs to come home with him."

"Can I see her?" Jason asked.

Sam handed the kitten over to Jason carefully, but the teen clearly knew how to hold her. He stroked her head gently as he examined her. "It doesn't look like anything's broken," he said. "She's probably just bruised. And hungry, from the looks of it. I wonder where her mum is."

"I don't know," Jeremy replied. "We didn't see any other cats in the sheds."

"They have free run of the station," Jason said. "They usually only go in the sheds when the weather's bad or to have their kittens. She doesn't look very old. I should see if I can find the rest of her litter. If she's in this kind of shape, the others might not be any better off."

"We found her caught in the next to the last gate on the right side of the sheds," Jeremy said. "That gives you a place to start at least."

"Thanks," Jason said. "I'll go find Seth, and we'll go hunting for them. Polly might be able to help too. She's always good at sniffing things out."

Jason ran off, whistling for his dog as he headed toward the machine shed where Sam had already learned Seth spent all of his spare time unless Patrick kicked him out or Jason dragged him off on one adventure or another.

"Should we go help?" Sam asked.

"No, let them have their fun," Jeremy said. "We'll introduce Little Bit to Arrow and get her settled, and then see what Kami has that we can give her. If you're going to keep her, you might want to think about getting some supplies from town. Cat food, a litter box, that sort of things. Even if she spends a lot of her time outside once she heals up, you want to have what you need instead of just improvising until she's well."

"Who has the next supply run?" Sam asked.

"I don't know, but we can find out," Jeremy said. "Do you have enough to cover it? If not, I can spot you a bit until payday."

"I think I can afford a bag of cat food and a litter box," Sam replied stiffly.

Jeremy sighed. "I wasn't trying to insult you or whatever. I just know you had to spend a lot of your last check on stuff for yourself. It's a friendly loan, nothing else."

"I know," Sam said. "I'm sorry. Money's a sensitive topic. When Alison and I agreed on a trial separation, I didn't have a job, so she said she'd pay for an apartment, but the amount she agreed to pay was barely enough to cover the rent in the cheapest place I could find, and I hardly had anything left over for food. I had some savings, but that only lasted a few months. I always felt like she was trying to use money as leverage to force me to come crawling back to her."

"It sounds like you're better off without her," Jeremy declared. "I don't blame you for getting rid of her."

Sam laughed, but the sound was bitter to his ears. "I'm pretty sure it was the other way around. There wasn't a lot I could do right as far as she was concerned."

"Then she was an idiot," Jeremy said, "because I have yet to see you do something wrong."

"Yeah, well, you don't have to live with me," Sam replied.

"I don't have to live with you," Jeremy agreed, "but I am living with you. Not in the same room, but we're under the same roof. We're spending most of our nonworking time together. Did you really spend that much more time with her when you were married?"

"Just sleeping in the same bed," Sam said. "With her schedule, we didn't even get to have dinner together half the time."

"Her loss," Jeremy said. "But I'm not going to complain since that means you're here now."

As they neared the bunkhouse, Arrow came bounding up to them and bumped Jeremy's leg with his head. Jeremy scratched the dog's ears affectionately. "Let's introduce them out here," Jeremy suggested. "That way if they don't get along, we can separate them more easily."

"Okay," Sam agreed.

Jeremy got a good grip on Arrow's collar and ordered him to sit. Arrow plopped his butt down and looked up at Jeremy adoringly. Sam couldn't help but smile at the expression. He knelt down so Arrow could see the kitten in his arms. She flattened her ears back and hissed, but Arrow ignored the warning, nosing her gently, but not, Sam noticed, near her sore ribs. She hissed a second time, although with less enthusiasm. Arrow responded by licking her face. She shook her head a couple of times, trying to dislodge the slobber that soaked her fur, but when she settled in his arms again, she was purring.

"I think he likes her," Jeremy said.

"I think it's mutual," Sam said when Arrow nudged her again and she tilted her head into the contact.

"Let's go see what Kami has for her," Jeremy suggested.

The kitten squirmed when Sam stood up, and Arrow yipped unhappily, so Sam set her down, poised to catch her if she stumbled or seemed in pain, but she wrapped around his ankles and then padded over to Arrow. He stood up as she walked between his front legs. She twined around his legs for a moment, with Arrow standing patiently.

"Or we could leave them together and go talk to Kami without them," Jeremy said with a smile.

"Maybe if Arrow comes with us, she'll follow," Sam said. "I'm not sure we should leave her alone yet."

"We can try," Jeremy said. "Heel, Arrow."

Arrow moved obediently to Jeremy's side, careful not to step on the kitten. She took a second to catch up, but before long, she was right between Arrow's legs again.

"At her pace, we'll never make it to the canteen," Jeremy said, scooping her up and setting her on Arrow's back. "Let's try this instead."

The kitten didn't seem to know what to make of that, turning around a couple of times to get her balance. Arrow stood perfectly still, patiently waiting for her to settle. She finally sat down on his back. As soon as she did, Arrow looked up at Jeremy as if to tell him they could go now.

"She's not going to be my cat. She's going to be his cat," Sam said.

"I'm sure he'll share," Jeremy replied with a grin.

They made it to the canteen with no problems. The kitten seemed perfectly content to sit on Arrow's back, and it didn't seem to bother Arrow to have her there. Sam figured Jeremy knew his dog well enough to know if it was a problem and to say something about it.

They left Arrow to cat-sit on the porch of the canteen and went in to find Kami.

"What did I tell you boys about disturbing me while I'm fixing dinner?" Kami snapped.

"We were hoping you'd have some scraps we could have," Sam said. "I found a kitten in the shed, and she's hurt and hungry. I'll get some cat food for her the next time someone goes to town, but I've got to take care of her until then. It doesn't have to be anything fancy. Just whatever you have left over."

Kami pursed his lips sourly, but Sam had already learned that was the cook's default expression, so he waited silently while Kami bustled around the kitchen. He came back with a thermos and a big bowl. "Keep that cold until you're ready to give it to her. You don't want the milk or the meat to spoil."

"Thank you," Sam said. "We'll get out of your way so you can finish dinner."

"If it's late, I'm telling everyone it's your fault for disturbing me."

"If it's late, we'll take the blame," Jeremy said.

They walked back outside with their goodies. Arrow had lain down on the porch, and the kitten was walking all over him. "She doesn't seem as sore as she was earlier," Jeremy said.

Sam picked her up, ignoring her yowl of protest. "Arrow can't stand up to carry you if you're on top of him," he told her. "Be patient a minute, and I'll let you go."

Arrow stood up immediately and woofed in Sam's direction. Sam returned the kitten to her perch on Arrow's back, and the strange little procession made its way back to the bunkhouse. Sam found a bowl and poured some of the milk into it. The kitten jumped off Arrow's back to investigate, eventually settling down to lap at the milk with a little pink tongue.

Sam cut the chicken innards into tiny pieces and put them on a plate next to the bowl. The kitten sniffed at them hesitantly. "It's okay, Little Bit," Sam said. "They're for you to eat. I know you're hungry."

She mewled at him and took a tentative taste. Sam couldn't imagine it tasting good, but she seemed to think it did, falling on the meal like she was starving. Then again, given her size, she probably was.

Jeremy came back with a cardboard box lined with newspaper. "Until we can set up a proper litter box for her, we should probably keep her in this while we're gone. We don't want to come back to messes all over the bunkhouse."

"You think she'll stay in that?" Sam asked.

"Not for very long," Jeremy said, "but we ought to get a couple of days out of it before she's healed enough and strong enough to jump out of it, and by then, we can figure out something better."

Sam wasn't convinced, but he figured it was worth a try, so when she had scarfed down all her food, he set her in the box. Immediately she started crying. Arrow whined in sympathy, sticking his head into the box and nudging her like he could figure out what was wrong. That seemed to calm her. Sam patted him on the head. "Keep an eye on our girl, okay, Arrow? We're going to eat dinner, and then we'll come back and let her out so you can play."

"I wonder if Jason found her litter mates," Jeremy said as they walked back to the canteen for dinner. The bell hadn't rung yet, but they weren't the only ones going in that direction.

"We can ask him at dinner," Sam said. "I hope they're okay and that she just got separated from them somehow."

"I hope so too," Jeremy said. "It's not like a mama cat to lose track of one of her kittens, though."

The expression on Jason's face when they entered the canteen and caught sight of him sitting in the corner didn't bode well for their fate, though.

"I found her den," Jason said when he saw them. "I don't know what predator found them, but the mum was pretty torn up, and there was no sign of any other kittens. I don't even know how many she had. We searched the shed and couldn't find any more, so I'm afraid whatever it was carried them all off."

"That's pretty brazen, isn't it? Coming into an inhabited area that way?" Sam asked. "I mean, I don't know a lot about wild animals, but that seems odd."

"Depends on what it was," Jason replied. "We've had owls nesting in the sheds before, and we found a wombat in one of the drover's huts in the spring. It's not common, exactly, but it's not unheard of either. If it was a bird of some kind, a falcon or a hawk or something, it could have been in and out when no one was around. Feral dogs don't usually make it this far down into the valley, but it's possible they did this time. Now that the breeding is done, we're not in there all that much."

"Is the mum going to make it?" Jeremy asked.

"It's too soon to know," Jason said. "I bandaged her up as best I could." He held up a hand covered in scratches. "Caine said he'd call the vet, but he can't get here until tomorrow. He's on an emergency call and can't come until that's sorted. I keep telling Caine we need to hire a vet of our own, but he says we don't have enough need to justify having one here all the time."

"You know he's right," Jeremy said gently. "There are times when a second vet in the area would be beneficial, but a lot of the time there isn't even enough work for Dr. Walker. He complains about it being feast or famine all the time."

"When I grow up, I'm going to be a vet, and I'm going to come back and work here," Jason said stubbornly. "Caine can hire me as a jackaroo and then pay me instead of another vet when he needs me."

"If you put all that work into getting your degree, you won't be satisfied just working as a jackaroo 90 percent of the time," Jeremy said. "It's a great plan, but don't lock yourself into it until after you get your degree and have a chance to think about it."

Jason's expression turned mulish, so Sam changed the topic to what they'd done for the kitten so far and how they intended to take care of her. Jason approved their choices, which shouldn't have made Sam feel as good as he did. Jason was a teenager, for heaven's sake, not a vet. Not yet.

When they finished dinner, Sam and Jeremy headed back to the bunkhouse. They opened the door and found Arrow sitting in front of the fireplace with the kitten curled up between his front paws, sound asleep. The box they had left her in was overturned on the other side of the room.

"Well, that didn't work," Sam said with a sigh. "I guess we'll have to think of something else." He bent to pick up the kitten, only to be discouraged by Arrow's deep growl. "Okay, maybe I'll just leave her there for now."

"Arrow," Jeremy scolded, "leave Sam alone. He's not going to hurt Little Bit."

"Oh, is that her name now?" Sam joked.

"It is until you come up with a better one," Jeremy said. "I can't just call her 'the kitten'."

"Arrow, come," Jeremy said. Arrow looked down at the kitten and back up at Jeremy, obviously torn between his desire to protect his charge and his obedience to his owner.

"Don't make him get up," Sam said. "They're not hurting anything, and it's cute how protective he is of her."

"She's going to be a pain in the arse," Jeremy muttered. "Completely spoiled already. I bet she whined until Arrow couldn't stand it and knocked the box over to get her out. She's not big enough to knock it over herself."

"Maybe he'll keep whatever made off with her siblings from grabbing her too," Sam said. "You want a beer or anything?"

"Sure," Jeremy said.

Sam smiled and went into the bunkhouse kitchen. Except for the kitten sleeping next to Arrow by the hearth, it was just like every night in the week since he'd moved into the bunkhouse, and Sam thought he could get used to this routine.

THIRTEEN

CAINE stared at the Google search in front of him. Sarah Armstrong was a much more common name than he'd anticipated. When he added Tumut into the search, nothing came up at all. He'd just have to check each name individually and see if he could narrow it down. Reminding himself that he had time, that he didn't need to be anywhere other than where he was on that cold, dreary May morning, he signed and started clicking on links, eliminating anyone under sixty-five. He didn't know how old Macklin's mother was when Macklin was born, but he figured sixty-five was a good cutoff. It put her in her early twenties when Macklin was born.

Two hours later, he had it narrowed down to seven possibilities based on age and not having anything else to eliminate the person as a choice. He'd left off one lady who was about the right age because she was a judge. Macklin hadn't even mentioned his mother working, and if she'd been a judge or even a lawyer at the time, surely she would have used her knowledge and connections to get away from Macklin's father. He'd eliminated another because she was aborigine, and the picture Macklin had of her showed she was clearly white. Mostly, though, with the women that age, there wasn't a lot of information. Name, city of residence, and little else. If he'd had her birth date, even without the year, he might have been able to narrow it down a little more, but he couldn't ask Macklin without revealing what he was doing, and he didn't want to say anything to Macklin until he knew more.

It took another two hours to chase down phone numbers for the seven women on his list, and by that point, he had to put it away for lunch. He hid the paper beneath a stack of old ledgers. If Sam found them, it wouldn't matter. Sam knew what Caine was doing. Macklin wouldn't touch the ledgers because he didn't want to mess up the system Sam and Caine had established since Sam started working in the office. Caine stood and stretched his back. Hiring Sam had been a stroke of genius. Now they just had to figure out how to keep him.

SAM was in the office when Caine returned after lunch, so Caine took a few minutes to discuss his progress and answer the questions that had come up as Sam worked on negotiating a new insurance policy to replace the one Uncle Michael had set up thirty years ago or more. When that was done, Caine took his list of names and went upstairs to his and Macklin's bedroom. The phone calls would be hard enough to make without someone listening in.

He looked at the list of names and his notes one more time and picked the woman he thought had the best chance of being Macklin's mother.

"Hello?"

"Is this Sarah Armstrong?"

"Yes, who is this?"

"My name is Caine Neiheisel. I run a sheep station in New South Wales. I'm trying to find the mother of my foreman, Macklin Armstrong."

"I'm sorry, son, but you've got the wrong Sarah Armstrong. My husband and I never had children."

"I'm sorry to have disturbed you," Caine said before ending the call.

The second call went almost exactly as the first, only that Sarah Armstrong had never married.

After striking out on the next call too, Caine wondered if he'd lost his mind, trying to do this without more information. He hid the list in his drawer under his clean socks and went outside to find Macklin. He'd already wasted enough of the day on a wild goose chase. He could call the rest another time.

"HEY, Sam," Jeremy said, sticking his head into the office. "I need to take Arrow out in the paddocks for a bit. Macklin wants to move one mob a little closer to the valley."

"Okay," Sam said, not sure why Jeremy was telling him this. Not that he minded knowing where Jeremy was, but it seemed odd that Jeremy would detour to find him.

"I need you to come get Little Bit," Jeremy said. "They both pitch a fit when I separate them. It helps if Little Bit is with you."

"I've got to come up with a better name for her," Sam said with a shake of his head, but he rose from the desk and followed Jeremy outside. Sure enough, the kitten was perched on Arrow's back, looking for all the world like she intended to go to work with Arrow and Jeremy.

He plucked her off Arrow's back, only to be met with a yowl of protest from her and a head-butt from Arrow. "Hey, you two," Sam said. "It's just for a few hours. Arrow, you can't watch her and do your work, and you, missy, are too small to go play with the big smelly sheep. They'd trample you without realizing it. You can sit in the office and play with my pens while I work."

"Thanks," Jeremy said. He called Arrow to him. Arrow went reluctantly, making Sam smile as he watched them head down the road toward the horses' paddock.

"Now that's a lovely sight, isn't it?" Caine said from behind him.

Sam felt himself blush all the way to the roots of his hair. "What do you mean?"

"A man and his dog," Caine said. "There's something special about that bond."

"I think Arrow is more interested in my kitten than in Jeremy these days," Sam said.

"What about you?" Caine asked. "What are you interested in these days?"

"Insurance premiums," Sam said with a grimace.

"That's not what I meant," Caine said. "As lovely a sight as man and dog are in the abstract, the look on your face wasn't very abstract."

"I can't even file for divorce for another six weeks," Sam said. "I'm not in any position to be interested in anyone at the moment."

"The heart doesn't work on any timeline," Caine said. "Don't let a good thing slip through your fingers because it's not the right time."

"It's not a question of the right time," Sam said. "I don't want to give Alison any ammunition."

"I thought you said you'd already agreed on the terms," Caine said.

"We did," Sam replied, "but that was before I had a job. If I don't give her any reason to want revenge, she probably won't try to make me pay her back for the money she spent on an apartment for me before I came up here. If I give her a reason, though, she could insist on a settlement of a different kind, and she'd probably win. She didn't have to support me for nine months before I got fed up with her and asked Neil for help, and if I've done something unsympathetic like had an affair with a man during our separation period, no judge is going to side with me."

"Jeremy's quite a catch," Caine said. "Worth waiting for. Just make sure he understands what's waiting for him too."

"We've talked about it," Sam said. "He said he understood."

"Then I won't say anything else about it," Caine said, "but if you ever need someone to talk to, I'm happy to listen."

"Thanks," Sam said. The kitten squirmed in his arms. "I'd better take her inside and get back to work."

Sam carried the kitten back into the office and closed the door so she couldn't go wandering through Caine and Macklin's house. She batted at the door with great dissatisfaction, but when it didn't open and no one came to help her, she gave a little huff and came back to Sam's feet. He bent down to scratch her ears, and she wrapped her little paws around his wrist so that when he straightened, she went with him. She jumped into his lap, circled around a couple of times, and plopped down across his thighs to begin grooming herself.

"Comfortable?" he asked with a smile.

She purred up at him and butted his hand.

"How am I supposed to work if you want to be patted?"

The look she gave him was supremely unconcerned. Sam just smiled and rested one hand on her tiny little back while he went back to entering data into the accounts with the other hand. If he was a little slower than he might have been with two hands, there was no one else in the room to notice, and the comfort of the kitten's purrs was more than worth the delay.

"See?" he said after a few minutes. "If you'd come in here with me instead of hanging out with Arrow all the time, you could spend all day like this, just relaxing and being held."

She rolled over, giving him access to her belly. He scratched obediently. "It's winter right now, so things are quieter, but when spring comes, Arrow's going to have to work a lot more. You're going to have to get used to him not being around during the day.'

She just purred louder.

"Of course that means I'm going to have to get used to Jeremy not being around as much during the day too," Sam said with a sigh. "We're a pair, aren't we? Mooning over a boy and his dog like this. At least we can spend the time together when they're out doing sheep-y type things."

It felt good to say the words, to admit that Jeremy had caught his interest beyond the friendship they were limited to until Sam's divorce went through. He couldn't budge on that, but he could use the next five months to lay a foundation on which to build something when the divorce was final and he was free.

He looked down at the kitten on his lap, heart pounding at the thought. "Oh God, I can't do this, can I? I've got to be out of my mind."

The kitten squirmed out from underneath his hands and braced her little paws on his chest, bumping her chin against his sternum. He picked her up and snuggled her closer. She purred and rubbed against his jaw. "Am I crazy to be thinking this way so soon?"

He took a deep breath to calm the reactionary panic. His marriage to Alison had been over for months now, even if the legal proceedings would take time to complete, so it wasn't like the idea of being single was new to him. He'd had nine months of thinking that way. Nine months of taking stupid chances in bars with nameless men for the sake of not feeling worthless for a few hours. He'd been at Lang Downs for six weeks already, long enough to have established a routine in his work and his downtime as well. He had always been a creature of habit, preferring to know how things would go ahead of time whenever possible, so having a new routine gave him a real sense of security, something that had been lacking since he lost his job. Separating from Alison had been almost easy in comparison. He'd spent four weeks with Jeremy, sharing evenings in the bunkhouse most nights, even if he did go to Neil and Molly's house at least once a week so Neil wouldn't feel like Sam was choosing Jeremy over him. Sam had invited Neil to the bunkhouse multiple times as well, but he'd always refused.

In those four weeks, Jeremy had been everything Sam could ask for in a friend. He'd been patient with Sam's ignorance about the workings of the station, understanding of Sam's obligations to work in the office, fun to be around, not to mention good for Sam's ego whenever he flirted a little or refused to let Sam put himself down. He was perfect, and that scared Sam a little. He'd learned the hard way that anything that looked too good to be true probably was.

He didn't want to start something with Jeremy only to have it end, because unlike his marriage with Alison, a relationship with Jeremy wouldn't be a sham to hide his sexuality from his father. A relationship with Jeremy would be the real thing, and losing that would be a hundred times harder than ending his marriage to Alison.

"What am I supposed to do, sweetheart?" he asked.

The kitten just purred up at him.

MACKLIN waited while Jeremy latched the gate behind them. It was a relief to have someone who knew what he was doing after a summer of herding jackaroos as much as sheep.

"How are you settling in?" Macklin asked when Jeremy drew up beside him again.

"Pretty well," Jeremy said. "It's nice having company in the bunkhouse, and Chris and Jesse invite me over a couple of times a week as well."

"That's good. The others are still giving you the cold shoulder?"

"Not everyone," Jeremy said. "Patrick and Carley have included me in a few things, and Ian asked me to help him out day before yesterday, even though I wasn't the only one available. I knew it wouldn't be easy coming here, but I'm not sorry I did."

"Good," Macklin said. "I can speak to Neil if you want."

"No, don't do that," Jeremy said. "You can order him to work with me, but you can't order him to be my friend, and even if you could, I wouldn't want you to. He has to come around in his own time."

"He can be stubborn," Macklin warned.

"So can I," Jeremy replied. "Right now, he's leaving me alone, and Molly is keeping him from giving Sam any grief about us being friends. I just don't want Sam to feel like he's caught in the middle."

"Oh, so that's the way it is," Macklin said with a grin.

"No, that's not the way anything is," Jeremy retorted, but Macklin saw the way Jeremy's skin darkened.

"Really?" Macklin said. "You know I'm not going to say anything about it, not when I ended up with Caine."

"It's not that," Jeremy said. "He's not ready for anything, and I'm not going to push him. His divorce isn't even final yet."

"It's a piece of paper," Macklin said. "They've already agreed to end the relationship."

"That's not the point," Jeremy said. "She's a bitch. I know I haven't met her and have only heard Sam's side of the story, but have you talked to him? Have you listened to the way he talks about himself? He doubts himself constantly. He thinks he's unattractive. He has no self-esteem. She did that to him, and I'm not going to give her anything else to use against him, whether in court or personally. When the divorce is final and he never has to talk to her again, it won't matter anymore, but right now, there's no way. She'd use anything between us as a blunt weapon to beat him to death, and I won't let that happen."

"You really think she would do that?" Macklin asked.

"It's not a chance I'm willing to take," Jeremy said, "and furthermore, it's not one Sam's willing to take. He's not thinking of it from an abuse perspective. He's thinking about it from a financial perspective. She supported him for nine months after they were separated. He's afraid she'll demand repayment if he gives her a reason to be annoyed with him."

"So we'd pay her off, and Sam could pay us back out of his salary," Macklin replied with a shrug.

"He'd never go for that," Jeremy said. "He's been dependent on her for so long that the thought of being dependent on anyone else scares him."

"You sure you want to take that on?" Macklin asked.

"I'm not planning on making him dependent on me," Jeremy said. "I'm hoping he'll learn he can rely on me, but he doesn't need someone to support him. He needs a partner. It's not the same thing."

"No, it's not," Macklin agreed, thinking about Caine and the station and the difference between working for Caine those first nine months and owning the station with him since Christmas. "You know him better than I do, but if there's anything Caine and I can do, one of you needs to tell us. We take care of our own at Lang Downs."

"I'm figuring that out," Jeremy said. "It's the piece of running a station Devlin never understood."

"In his defense, your father wasn't a lot better," Macklin said. "Devlin didn't have the same model for running a station that I did."

"Caine didn't have any model," Jeremy retorted.

"Caine is... Caine," Macklin said finally, not sure how else to describe his lover. "He doesn't play by any rules but his own."

"He's one hell of a man," Jeremy agreed. "You're a lucky son of a bitch."

Macklin laughed. "Don't I know it."

"So tell me about this horse of yours," Jeremy said. Macklin allowed the change of subject because it was easier than talking about his emotions. That was Caine's area of expertise, not his.

"What about him?" Macklin asked.

"I keep hearing no one can ride him but you."

"That's not completely true," Macklin said. "He let Michael ride him before Michael got too frail to have any business on horseback."

"Why?"

"Why did he let Michael ride him? Or why won't he let anyone else?" Macklin asked.

"Both," Jeremy said.

"We bought him at an auction," Macklin said. "A mob of brumbies that was going to be put down if they couldn't be sold or relocated. Michael was furious. He wanted to relocate the whole mob, but we couldn't afford it, and other people were bidding on them, so he let them go to other stations. Then Ned came up, screaming and fighting, and so clearly not the kind of horse you could throw a saddle on and put straight to work. Michael got him for almost nothing, far less than he was worth."

"If he can't be ridden, he isn't worth a whole lot," Jeremy said.

"Really?" Macklin said. "Is Sam worth less because he's not free right now or because he has issues you'll have to work through?"

"What? Of course not!"

"Then why shouldn't the same be true of Ned?"

"Because Ned's a business investment," Jeremy said.

"The same way Arrow is a business investment?"

"He's useful, at least."

"So is Ned," Macklin said. "He's the most reliable horse I've ever ridden."

"So you bought him at a brumby auction, wild as can be," Jeremy said. "I guess you broke him or Lang did?"

"Neither," Macklin said. "He'd already been broken. You can see it in the scars all over his sides. We helped him heal, and we let him come to us, and once he did, we taught him what kindness meant. He trusts us because we've never raised a hand to him. He doesn't trust anyone else because he has no reason to. Most of the year-rounders have favorite horses of their own, so they don't need to ride him. Caine doesn't ride well enough to handle a horse as strong as Ned. And it works wonders for my reputation with the seasonal jackaroos to see me riding him like it's nothing when most of them can't even get on his back, much less stay there."

Jeremy chuckled. "Okay, I can see that part. It just seems risky. What if someone needed to ride him? Not just to prove a point or anything, but actually needed to."

"I don't know," Macklin said. "We'd have to hope for the best."

FOURTEEN

CAINE had to wait almost a week before he got a chance to make the remaining calls to the women he'd identified, hoping one of them might be Macklin's mother. Macklin wanted Caine's opinion on this and that and the other thing, and Caine could hardly complain when the whole point of hiring Sam was to have more freedom for himself to go out into the paddocks with Macklin and to work on the organic certification for the station. The list of names had haunted him, though, and finally there was a day when Macklin didn't have something specific he needed Caine for, so Caine gave the excuse of checking in with Sam for a few hours to get the time alone.

He made two more calls that ended in disappointment. He had two names left, and then he'd have to go back and start the search over. Hoping for the best, he dialed the second-to-last number and waited for an answer.

"Hello?"

"May I speak with Sarah Armstrong, please?"

"Speaking."

"Mrs. Armstrong, my name is Caine Neiheisel."

"Is this a sales call?"

"No, ma'am, I'm trying to find someone, and I'm hoping you can help me."

"I'm pretty sure I can't," the woman said. "No one would want to find me, and I don't know anyone worth finding."

As miserable as that sounded, it gave Caine hope. "Does the name Macklin mean anything to you?"

"Not anymore."

She sounded so sad that Caine was sure he'd found the woman he was looking for. "He misses you, Mrs. Armstrong."

"You know Macklin?"

"I do," Caine said. "He's my partner."

Mrs. Armstrong was silent for so long Caine wondered if he'd lost the connection.

"What kind of partner?" she asked finally.

Caine nearly cried in relief. He'd thought from Macklin's comments that his mother had guessed about his sexuality, but he hadn't been sure. "Both kinds," he said. "We own a sheep station in New South Wales."

"Is he… is he happy?"

"I l-like to think so," Caine said, silently cursing his stutter, but his emotions were too high to control it. "He's a w-wonderful m-m-man."

"I'm glad," she said. "His father was a miserable bastard who made both our lives hell. Macklin got out, thank God, but by the time his father died, I didn't have any way to find him."

"W-would you l-l-like to see him again?" Caine asked.

"You have no idea how much," she said, and he could hear tears in her voice. "I've worried about him and prayed for him. I never believed I'd see him again."

Caine considered his options for a moment. Getting Macklin away from the station for long would be a challenge, but depending on where his mother was, Caine could pick her up and bring her back to the station for a visit. "Where are you living now?" he asked, because he hadn't bothered to write down addresses along with the phone numbers. "Perhaps I could come pick you up, and you could come to the station for a visit."

"In Canberra," she said. "I left Tumut after my husband died."

"That's only an hour and a half from Boorowa," Caine said. "Our station is north of there. When would you like to come?"

"I'm still working," Mrs. Armstrong said. "I don't have another long weekend until the Queen's Birthday in June."

Caine checked his calendar, glad it had the Australian holidays marked or he wouldn't have known the Queen's birthday was celebrated on the second Monday of June. "I'll be there the Friday before," Caine said. "We'll drive as far as Boorowa after you get off work and then decide if you're up to the drive to the station that night or if you'd rather stay in Boorowa and drive the rest of the way in the morning."

"Bless you, child," Mrs. Armstrong said. "You're a miracle worker."

"No, ma'am, nothing like that."

"Please, call me Sarah."

Caine smiled. "I'll see you in a month, Sarah." He gave her his phone number and e-mail in case she needed to reach him before then and hung up. He leaned back against the headboard and smiled. It would be the perfect surprise for Macklin.

SAM sat on the porch of the bunkhouse, watching his kitten—he really had to name her soon or she'd be Little Bit forever—chase a leaf around the grassy area between the bunkhouse and the road. She wasn't moving stiffly anymore, but with her mum still in no shape to take care of her, Sam had given up the idea of sending her back to the sheds, which meant she needed a name. A real name.

"What are we going to call her?" Sam asked when Jeremy joined him on the porch and handed him a beer.

"Little Bit," Jeremy said like it was the most obvious choice in the world.

"That's a nickname, not a real name," Sam said. "She needs something dignified."

She tumbled arse over head, surprising a laugh from both of them. "Yeah, like she's so dignified."

"She'll grow out of the awkward kitten stage," Sam said, "and for all you know, she'll end up weighing twenty pounds, and then won't that name seem silly?"

A screech overhead made them look up. A hawk, to judge by the size, glided over the valley.

"I still haven't got used to seeing them," Sam said. "We didn't have a lot of hawks or other big birds in Melbourne."

"No, you wouldn't," Jeremy said. "They need rodents and the like to hunt, and that's easier to do up here than in a city. I'd see one occasionally in uni, but almost always near a park of some kind."

The hawk screeched again, diving toward the grass in the distance. "He's found something," Jeremy said. "I wonder what he caught."

When the hawk began its ascent, talons empty, Sam said, "Nothing, apparently."

"He'll try again," Jeremy said. "He's hunting, no doubt about it."

The hawk circled overhead a few more times and dove again, this time almost directly at them. Sam never saw where Arrow came from, but fur and feathers collided when the hawk tried to grab the kitten. Arrow leaped at the bird, knocking it from the air and away from the kitten. He stood over her protectively, barking and snarling at the stunned predator but not moving an inch from his post.

The hawk righted itself after a moment, shaking out its feathers. It glared at Arrow but didn't challenge him. Arrow barked again and that was enough. The hawk launched itself skyward again, flying toward the far end of the valley.

"I guess it thought she was easy pickings," Sam said slowly, his heart pounding in his chest.

"If he got the rest of her family, he probably didn't see any reason not to go after the one that got away," Jeremy replied just as slowly. "Come here, Arrow."

Arrow turned his head in Jeremy's direction but didn't budge.

"It's okay, Arrow," Sam said. "The hawk is gone now."

Arrow looked at them like they'd both lost their minds, but he stepped back so the kitten was in front of him instead of between his legs and nudged her toward the porch. She went happily enough, scampering up the steps with Arrow right behind her.

Sam reached down and picked her up, checking to make sure the hawk's talons hadn't scratched her before Arrow got there, but he couldn't find any trace of blood on her fur. "I know what her name is," Sam said.

"What?"

"Hawk."

Jeremy smiled and scratched her head. "If you say so."

Sam looked down at her precious little face and smiled too. "I do."

"HEY, mates," Seth said, all but bouncing as he ran into the bunkhouse holding a box. "Can I hide this in here?"

"What is it?" Jeremy asked suspiciously. "And why are you hiding it?"

"It's a surprise for Chris," Seth said. "His birthday is today, and this is for the party tonight. He knows we're having a party, but he doesn't know I got him a present. Patrick picked it up when he went in to town yesterday. He just got back."

"So what did you get him?" Sam asked.

"No way, not telling" Seth said. "If you want to know what it is, you have to come to the party tonight."

"Everyone would have more fun if I stayed here," Jeremy said.

"Sam wouldn't," Seth said.

"That's not fair, Seth," Sam scolded. "You shouldn't make Jeremy feel guilty for not wanting to be in a room full of people who don't want anything to do with him."

"Chris doesn't feel that way," Seth insisted. "Jesse and I don't feel that way. You come over to the house all the time. Patrick and Carley don't feel that way. They invite you over every time they do something. The only ones who feel that way are Neil, Ian, and Kyle, and Ian and Kyle probably only feel that way because Neil does."

"The fact remains that if I'm there, Neil, Ian, and Kyle will spend the evening scowling at me and generally ruining your brother's party," Jeremy said.

"Nope, not accepting it," Seth said. "If they want to ruin the party, we'll make them leave."

"I appreciate the support, Seth, but I promised Macklin I wouldn't turn his station into a war zone."

"So don't," Seth said. "Come to the party, drink a few beers, and have a good time. If they make a big deal out of it, they're the ones causing problems, not you."

"I'll take care of Neil," Sam said before Jeremy could argue more. "He likes Chris. He'll play nice so he doesn't ruin Chris's birthday as long as someone makes him think about it before he gets there. Molly and I will keep him in line."

"Thanks," Jeremy said.

"I'll go find him now," Sam said, "and I'll see you both at the party later."

Sam left the bunkhouse and went in search of Neil. Fortunately nobody had been sent out into the upper paddocks that day, so there was a limit to where Neil could be. Sam found him in the sheds repairing worn leather on some of the station's bridles.

"Hi, Sam," he said when he heard Sam come in.

"Hi," Sam said. "Got a minute?"

"Sure," Neil said. "This has to be done, but it's not something that requires a lot of concentration. What's going on?"

"Seth and Jesse planned a birthday party for Chris tonight," Sam said.

"Yes, I know. They invited everyone," Neil said.

"Yes," Sam agreed. "They invited everyone. That includes Jeremy."

Neil frowned.

"And that's why I'm here," Sam said. "To remind you not to act that way tonight. You don't have to talk to Jeremy, but you can't spend the evening glaring at him. When it's your birthday, you can choose not to invite him, but Chris wants him there, and you can't spoil Chris's party just because you don't like him."

"I wouldn't do that," Neil protested.

"Not on purpose," Sam agreed. "I know you'd never do it on purpose, but if you aren't thinking about it, you'll act the same way you do at dinner every night, and that would spoil the mood of the party. Just don't scowl at him, okay?"

"I'll try," Neil said. "If I forget, remind me."

"I will," Sam said, "and I'll tell Molly to do the same." He hesitated for a moment before continuing. "You know, I really think you'd like him if you'd give him a chance. You have so much in common. The only thing keeping you apart is his last name."

"I just don't understand why he's here," Neil said.

"Because his brother kicked him off Taylor Peak," Sam replied. "You'll have to ask him why. That's not my story to tell, at least without his permission. I know you can't imagine a situation that would make us fall out like that, and really I can't either, but Devlin isn't either of us. He's more like Dad, and I can think of plenty of situations that would have made Dad wash his hands of either one of us."

"Yeah, I suppose that's true," Neil said. "I'll try to tone it down. It's just I have reason not to trust Taylor."

"Which Taylor?" Sam pressed. "Have you ever actually had a problem with Jeremy? Or has it always been with his brother?"

Neil hesitated for a moment. "I guess it's always been with Devlin or with his jackaroos. Now that I think about it, I don't remember Jeremy ever being involved in any of the dustups."

"Then try to give him the benefit of the doubt," Sam asked. "He's done that and more for me."

"I'll try," Neil said.

WHEN they got to the canteen for dinner, Sam had to smile. Seth and Jesse had outdone themselves. The canteen was draped with streamers and a huge banner proclaiming that Chris was turning twenty-one. Kami had a huge spread laid out, far more than the year-rounders could eat, but that didn't seem to matter. He'd made all of Chris's favorite dishes, set out buffet style. Sam figured they'd be enjoying Chris's birthday dinner for a week.

"Did you talk to Neil?" Jeremy asked softly when Sam joined him.

"I did," Sam said. "He promised to be on his best behavior for Chris. It'll be fine. You'll see. Let's grab a plate before the rissoles are gone." Sam had already learned that Kami's rissoles were everyone's favorite.

Patrick and Carley joined them at the table after they'd all heaped their plates high with food. Sam had given up trying to eat less since he'd gotten to the station. Kami's cooking was too good, for one thing. For another, everyone scolded him for not eating enough. He'd worried about gaining weight, but Jeremy had been true to his word about teaching Sam to ride, and that seemed to be enough exercise to keep the weight off, so Sam had stopped worrying about it.

"Seth and Jason have a whole playlist set up for the party," Carley told them. "It's been a huge discussion at our house the past week, in between their lessons. Which songs, which order, what's sure to make Chris and Jesse have a dance… you'd think this was rocket science, not music."

"Music is very serious business when you're sixteen," Sam said.

"Fifteen and seventeen, but I suppose you're right," Carley said. "I have to remind myself of all the mix tapes we used to make and share when I was in high school."

Jeremy laughed. "You're dating yourself there, Carley."

"I have a fifteen-year-old son. Nobody thinks I'm from anything other than the Stone Age."

"Lies," Patrick said. "A pack of bloody lies. You can't possibly be a day over twenty."

Carley sent her husband a fond look and turned back to Sam and Jeremy. "You should dance tonight too."

"You and Molly are going to be in high demand," Jeremy replied. "You're outnumbered."

"Oh, I didn't mean with me," Carley said. "You should dance with each other. Nobody here will care."

"Maybe not," Sam said, "but I'm not sure it's a good idea."

"Why not?" Carley demanded.

"Because my divorce isn't final," Sam said.

"It's a dance, not a marriage proposal," Carley scoffed. "You're not breaking any laws by enjoying yourself with a friend."

Alison wouldn't see it that way if she found out, but Sam didn't want to say that aloud. He already knew Jeremy's opinion of her. He didn't need everyone else's as well.

As soon as most people had finished eating, Seth and Jason set up the stereo and started the music and their demands that Chris and Jesse (and anyone else who wanted to join them) get up and dance. Chris didn't look convinced, but Jesse grabbed his hand and pulled him into the center of the room, where tables had been pushed back for this very purpose.

The dance was awkward, neither of them knowing how to follow well, but Sam could see the easy affection between them, and the smiles on everyone else's faces assured him that Carley was right and no one cared that two men were dancing together.

The song ended, and Seth yelled, "Who's next in line to dance with the birthday boy?"

No one moved for a minute, and then Kyle, one of the jackaroos who'd helped Macklin save Chris's life, stood up. "Why the hell not?" he said. "It *is* his birthday."

Everyone laughed, and before long, Ian cut in on Kyle, spinning Chris around the dance floor with far more style than Kyle or Jesse had managed. When Neil cut in a few minutes later, Sam let out a huge sigh. He still couldn't believe how far Neil had come. Molly cut in after that, leaving Chris looking incredibly uncomfortable until she took pity on him and started leading too. Before long, almost everyone in the room had taken a turn.

"Go on," Jeremy said, nudging Sam toward the dance floor. "It's his birthday."

"You haven't danced with him either," Sam said.

"Dance with him, and then I will," Jeremy promised. "And then I'll dance with you."

Sam hesitated over the last piece of the offer, but some of the others were dancing together, even ones who weren't couples and weren't even gay as far as Sam knew, so he thought maybe it would be okay. Everyone else would think it was the same as Kyle and Ian dancing, or everyone dancing with Chris. He didn't really think Alison had spies on the station since she couldn't have expected him to come up here before he did it, and no one new had arrived since he got here, but if word did somehow get back to her about the party, he could insist the dance with Jeremy was just another dance, not something so much more.

He weaved through the dancers until he could cut in on Carley dancing with Chris. She ceded her place with a smile and a laugh. Chris grinned at him. "I wondered how long it would take you to come out here."

"I'm not much of a dancer," Sam said.

"And any of the rest of us are?" Chris retorted. "It's not about the dancing. It's about having fun."

It was fun, Sam had to admit. He'd expected to feel self-conscious about dancing in general and about dancing with a man in particular, but nobody was staring at them. Nobody was laughing or sneering. Everybody else was having fun too, in much the same way. Sam let himself relax and enjoy. Jeremy cut in far too soon.

Sam took a step back and let Jeremy and Chris spin away from him. Before he could feel awkward about standing there, Molly grabbed his hand. "My turn," she said. "So are you going to dance with Jeremy?"

"You're the third person tonight to ask me that," Sam said.

"You're not exactly subtle about the way you watch him, sweetie," Molly said. "It's safe here, remember?"

"Nowhere's really safe," Sam said. "Not until the divorce is final."

"If you were sleeping with him, that might be true," Molly said, "but you're not worried about dancing with me. Why should you worry about dancing with him?"

"Because I'm not attracted to you," Sam said.

"It's a dance, Sam, nothing more. Besides, unless you told your ex about you, she's far more likely to have an issue with you dancing with another woman than with a man," Molly pointed out. "You're seeing everything funny because you have a secret, but most people don't look at the world through that prism."

"You figured it out."

"No, Neil told me," Molly said. "I figured out about Jeremy, but only because I was watching for it. Caine might have noticed because he sees things through the same prism and because he's a hopeless romantic who wants everyone to be as happy as he is. Seth and Jason might have seen it because those two are more precocious than is good for them, but I'd bet none of the others have, not unless Jeremy has said something to them."

"I don't think he has," Sam replied. "He's not any more out than I am, really."

"Is he willing to be?" Molly asked sharply.

"I think so," Sam said. "He said he told Macklin the first day, and I'm pretty sure his brother knows, although I'm not sure Devlin will spread it around since he'd see it as reflecting on him."

Molly rolled her eyes. "Spare me the stupidity of Aussie stockmen."

"Hey, they're not all bad," Sam protested. "You're marrying one, remember?"

"And he's the worst of the bunch," she muttered, "although he did dance with Chris tonight, and he hasn't scowled at Jeremy once."

"He might if I agree to dance with Jeremy," Sam said.

"You dance with Jeremy. I'll deal with Neil," Molly said. "There, he's free. Go grab him before someone else does."

Sam took a deep breath and started toward where Jeremy was standing. He could have sworn every eye in the room turned his way, but when he dared to glance around, no one seemed to have noticed his progress across the room.

No one, that is, except Jeremy. Jeremy had fixated on him from the moment he let go of Molly. Sam couldn't decide if he wanted to run to Jeremy or turn and run away. The intensity of the look on Jeremy's face made him nervous. He'd gotten used to hanging out with Jeremy, to being his buddy, but Jeremy wasn't looking at him like a buddy now. Jeremy was looking at him like a treat he intended to devour whole.

Sam swallowed hard and made his feet keep moving in Jeremy's direction. No one had ever looked at him like that, and he hadn't the slightest idea what to do with the emotions it churned up inside him. They couldn't do this. He still had another month before he could even file for divorce, and at least three months after that before it was finalized.

He very nearly turned and ran in the other direction. He couldn't do this. Not now, maybe not ever, but before he could panic, Jeremy smiled, and Sam smiled back because he couldn't help it. Then he was at Jeremy's side, and Jeremy was pulling him into an embrace and guiding him onto the dance floor.

They were all but the same height. Jeremy had maybe an inch on Sam, but not enough to make dancing together awkward, not like it had seemed when Macklin danced with Jason, who hadn't hit his growth spurt yet. It also meant that Jeremy's blue-green eyes were right there in Sam's line of sight, mesmerizing in the swirl of color. Sam blinked a couple of times, but the central ring of a slightly different color wasn't a figment of his imagination. Neither was the way Jeremy was looking at him. Sam nearly stumbled, but Jeremy steadied him with those big hands Sam refused to let himself fantasize about. The one that held his between their chests was gentle, the grip firm but not painful, the calluses on Jeremy's palm evident with his fingers curled around Sam's. The other hand rested at his waist, not quite pulling him close—they weren't a couple, after all—but definitely holding him. Sam could feel the heat of it radiating through his shirt. And the look on Jeremy's face, all hot and possessive, like he wanted to wrap Sam up in his arms and never let go… Sam shook with need at the sight of that look directed at him.

"This is a bad idea," Sam said hoarsely.

"No, it isn't," Jeremy replied. "It's the best idea I've ever had. Don't run from me, Sam. I'm not asking for anything but a dance, not until you're ready, but don't deny us this."

Sam swallowed hard, heat flushing through him. He was sure his cheeks were the color of tomatoes, but he nodded and kept dancing. Their thighs brushed together as they danced, leaving Sam torn between pulling back and pressing closer. He had seen Jeremy ride. He knew what kind of muscles lurked beneath his jeans. He wanted those legs pressed against his own, pressed between his own. He wanted to push forward and rut against Jeremy until he couldn't think of anything else. He was so tired of trying to keep it together, of always worrying about everything. The siren's call of a few hours of oblivion in Jeremy's arms was strong, and Sam knew Jeremy would give it to him. It would only take a word from him and Jeremy would take charge, take him back to the bunkhouse, and make him feel good in a way none of the hookups in Melbourne ever had. Even better, Jeremy would still be there in the morning, looking at him with the same heat in his eyes, the same offer of friendship, companionship, and more.

It would be so easy and feel so good, but in the morning, Jeremy would want more, and right now, Sam couldn't afford to give it to him. He had to push those yearnings aside, push them back down until he was free of Alison. If Jeremy still wanted him then, Sam would take everything he could get and be grateful for it. He just had to wait four more months.

When the song was over, he took a step back, resisting the urge to go outside to cool off. It had just been a dance, so why did he feel like he'd been split open and remade? "Thanks for the dance," he said awkwardly, knowing he was running away but unable to stop himself.

"You're welcome," Jeremy said and then let him go.

Sam had never been more grateful in his life.

"You okay?" Neil asked when he found Sam sitting in the corner a few minutes later.

"Yeah."

"Really? Because you look like you either saw a ghost or that bloody hawk finally made off with your cat," Neil said.

"No, it's just...."

"Just what?" Neil prompted.

"Let's go for a walk," Sam said. He didn't know how Neil would react, and he didn't want to make a scene at Chris's party.

Neil nodded and followed him outside. The wind was cold off the tablelands, and Sam shivered, wishing he'd grabbed his jacket before he came to the party. It was too late now, though.

"Promise me you'll let me finish before you say anything," Sam said.

"I'm not going to like this, am I?" Neil asked.

"Probably not," Sam said, "but I need you to really listen to me instead just blowing up at me."

"Okay, I'm listening."

"You are so in love with Molly," Sam began. "You can't imagine that going sour, and I hope it never does for you. You can't imagine what it feels like to have the person who's supposed to be the closest to you in the world turn on you and say things that make you doubt yourself. And then say them so often and so harshly that you can't do anything but believe her."

"Alison—"

"Don't interrupt," Sam spat. "This is hard enough as it is. She made me think I wasn't good for anything. She made me think nobody would ever want me and she was doing me a favor by keeping me around. She made me think...." He took a deep breath. "It doesn't matter what she made me think. The point is, my marriage was a living hell, and by the time I got here, I just wanted to curl up in a dark corner and be left alone. Except nobody would let me do that, least of all Jeremy."

Neil opened his mouth, but Sam glared at him until he shut it again.

"Jeremy has spent the past six weeks being my friend, kicking me in the arse when I start feeling sorry for myself, and basically doing everything he can to make me feel better about myself, and he's done it without expecting anything from me in return except my friendship," Sam said. "He isn't pushing for anything else because he knows I'm not ready and the divorce isn't final."

"Wait—"

"Shut up," Sam snapped. "I know you don't like him, but I do, Neil. I like him a bloody lot, and for some unknown reason, he seems to feel the same about me, and it's freaking me out a bit. I don't know how to do this. The only serious relationship I've ever had was with Alison, and you see how that turned out."

"Bloody hell, you're going to make me accept a Taylor as part of my family, aren't you?" Neil said.

Sam choked back a laugh. "Out of everything I just told you, that's what you fixate on?"

Neil shrugged. "That's the easiest part to deal with. The rest makes me want to punch someone."

"As long as it's not Jeremy or me, you can punch whoever you want."

"Alison was the primary candidate," Neil said. "So Taylor's gay too? Is that why he's here?"

"Yeah," Sam said. "I'm not sure if his brother found out or if Jeremy just got sick of listening to him, but it's why he left."

"And you're sure he's who you want?"

"Neil—"

"No, I swear, I'm not saying that because of who it is," Neil said quickly. "You said yourself you've never had a serious relationship except with Alison. Your divorce isn't even finalized yet, although that can't happen soon enough after everything you just told me. This isn't about Taylor or how I feel about him. I just want to make sure you aren't rushing into something you'll regret later. Rebound relationships and all that."

Sam considered Neil's question for a moment before answering. "Life doesn't come with guarantees, but I know what a bad relationship feels like. I know what I don't want. A lot of guys, the guys I hooked up with in Melbourne, wouldn't care that I was still legally married, even if we're separated. A lot of guys wouldn't have the patience to deal with my concerns about what Alison will do if she finds out I'm gay and involved with someone else before it's over. A lot of guys—"

"You haven't been hanging out with the right guys," Neil interrupted. "Tell me about Taylor."

"You could start by calling him by his name," Sam said. "He's kind. Maybe that doesn't sound like a lot, but to me, it's huge. He's patient and funny and he makes me laugh. He makes me forget I'm not part of this place in the way the rest of you are."

"What do you mean you aren't part of Lang Downs the way the rest of us are?"

"I'm not a jackaroo," Sam said. "I won't ever be a jackaroo. I'm not naïve. Jeremy doesn't seem to care about that, though. He talks to me like I know what he's talking about and might actually have an opinion. He explains things to me when I ask. He's teaching me to ride. He lets me work with his dog."

"All of those things are great," Neil said. Sam scowled at him. "No, I mean that. Really. But belonging on Lang Downs isn't about being a jackaroo. Patrick isn't. Sure, he can ride a horse if he has to, but he's a mechanic, not a sheep herder."

"Yeah, but the station needs a mechanic."

"The station also needs someone to keep the books and make sure we all get paid," Neil reminded him. "Caine didn't invent a job for you."

"Jeremy looks at me like I'm worth something," Sam said softly. "He looks at me like he thinks he's lucky to have me."

"He is."

"You're my brother. You're biased," Sam said, but he smiled as he did. "Nobody else ever has. Alison didn't even think that when I had a job and was contributing to the household. Once I lost my job, I wasn't worth her time unless it was to yell at me. The men in Melbourne didn't even see me. Not really. They saw a way to get their rocks off. In their defense, I didn't really see them either. Jeremy, though, he sees me, and he still looks at me that way."

"Damn, I guess I'd better get used to calling him Jeremy, hadn't I?"

FIFTEEN

NEIL went back to the party after they finished talking, but Sam's mood had shifted. He wouldn't be good company now and didn't want to inflict his contemplative mood on anyone else. He walked back to the bunkhouse and found his Driza-Bone. It was a beautiful night, with the stars bright overhead, so Sam went back out to the veranda and leaned on the railing as he stared up at the night sky. The moon hadn't risen or had already set, Sam didn't know which, so he could see the full wash of stars. The majesty of it took his breath away.

"Hey there," Jeremy said, coming up the road from the canteen. "You didn't come back to the party. I got worried about you."

"I'm okay," Sam said. A smile broke over his face as he realized it was true. "I had a chat with Neil. He invited us to have dinner with him and Molly on Sunday."

"Your brother, the one who hates me, invited us to have dinner with him? What did you say to him?"

"I told him about Alison, about you, about everything, pretty much," Sam admitted. "I told him you looked at me like I was worth something."

"You are worth something," Jeremy insisted.

"Yeah, he agrees with you," Sam said, "but the fact you feel that way won him over, or started to, anyway."

"I thought we were waiting until your divorce is final to start anything," Jeremy said.

"We are," Sam said, "but I didn't need to wait another four months to start getting him used to the idea of having you around."

"I thought we were waiting until your divorce was final to see where we stand," Jeremy amended.

"We were," Sam said, "but I realized tonight that I don't need another four months to know what I want. I might have to wait to have it, and I know you might change your mind or not be ready to make up your mind, but I am, and I needed to share that with Neil."

Jeremy stepped into Sam's space, telegraphing every movement before he made it, but Sam had no desire to pull away. If anything, he moved closer, into the kiss. Jeremy's lips were chapped and rough against Sam's, but the kiss itself was almost unbearably tender, like Sam had handed Jeremy the fulfillment of every wish on a single platter, and Jeremy just couldn't help himself. Jeremy lifted one hand to cradle Sam's jaw, his fingers warm against Sam's cool cheek. Sam could feel Jeremy's calluses against his skin, the touch reminding him who he was with and how incredibly lucky he was to be here. He shuddered with the enormity of it.

Jeremy broke the kiss, resting his forehead against Sam's. "You okay there, mate?"

Sam wanted to nod and assure Jeremy he was fine, but he couldn't. He was quaking, but he couldn't explain why. Jeremy tipped his head, rubbing their noses together. "No pressure, Sam. I swear, but after what you said…. I'm sorry if I moved too fast."

Sam took a deep breath. He didn't want to pull away. The way Jeremy was holding him, their foreheads touching, their noses brushing and breath mingling, was almost unbearably intimate, more than all the sex he'd had in the back rooms of bars or seedy hotel rooms, more even than the years he had spent living with Alison. Even before things got bad between them, it had never been like this.

"I… don't know how to do this," Sam said with a shaky breath.

"Do what?" Jeremy asked.

"Anything, it feels like," Sam said, laughing bitterly.

"That's not what it looks like from where I'm standing," Jeremy said, drawing Sam inside the bunkhouse, where it was warmer. Instead of letting Sam retreat to the chair by the huge stone fireplace where he usually sat, Jeremy pulled Sam with him to the couch. "You convinced your brother not to make a scene at Chris's party. You told him about us. You stood up for yourself, since I'm sure he wasn't happy about the news."

"Actually, his biggest concern was that I was rushing into something before I was ready for it," Sam said, "not who I was rushing into it with."

"That's... surprising," Jeremy said slowly. "I would have expected more of a reaction from him."

"Either you've been winning him over without realizing it, or he's even more loyal to me than I realized," Sam said.

"So what happens now?" Jeremy asked.

"What do you mean?"

"Your divorce still won't be final until September, and it's only the end of May, no matter how much I might wish otherwise," Jeremy said. "I couldn't let the moment pass without kissing you, but I made some promises to you, and I don't intend to break them."

"Good," Sam said, still feeling like his head was spinning. "I don't know what happens now. I guess we keep doing the same things we've already been doing, except maybe we spend a little more time with Neil and Molly. I really do think you could be friends if you give each other a chance."

"For you, I'd give the devil himself a chance," Jeremy said. "Neil's a hothead. When I still lived at Taylor Peak, I always assumed he was a hotheaded jerk and wondered why Macklin kept him around, but I've seen him work since I've been here, and I've seen him with you. He's a hothead, but he's not a jerk."

"No, he's not," Sam agreed. He leaned against Jeremy's shoulder. "I don't think we should kiss very often because it's so easy for that to turn into wanting more, but sitting with you like this is nice."

"It is nice," Jeremy agreed, shifting so he could put his arm around Sam's shoulders. Sam scooted closer until their sides touched. "There's a lot more to a relationship than just sex. We can spend the next three or four months building the rest, and when your divorce is final and we can actually have sex, the waiting will make it even better."

"Why do I feel like a virgin waiting for her wedding night?" Sam asked.

"Don't know," Jeremy said with a shrug and a smile, "but I'm not going to complain about being the one you pick."

"You know I'm not really a virgin."

"I didn't think you were," Jeremy said, "but I still like being the one you pick to be with."

Sam smiled and snuggled a little closer. A part of him wished his divorce was already final so they didn't have to worry about what happened next, but even with that shadow lingering over them, Sam couldn't imagine being anywhere other than right where he was.

JEREMY lay in bed late that night, his cold, lonely bed, thank you very much, and tried to will away the arousal that had been on a low, slow burn since he'd found Sam on the veranda. Unfortunately his imagination was stronger than his willpower. He tossed and turned restlessly on his narrow bunk, thankful that Lang Downs had a bunkhouse with separate rooms for each jackaroo. They weren't fancy, but they had walls and a door and at least the illusion of privacy. Even better, Sam has chosen a room on the other side of the common area, so the chances of him hearing if Jeremy gave in and dealt with the problem were slim.

He closed his eyes and called up the image of Sam on the veranda, so open and innocent as Jeremy kissed him the first time. The whole virgin conversation aside, Sam was innocent in so many ways. He'd been beaten up by life a bit, but he hadn't turned cold and bitter. And he'd kissed Jeremy like it was the most wondrous thing in the world. That was good for Jeremy's ego, but it also proved his point. That chaste, tender kiss shouldn't have been anything special, yet it clearly had been. Jeremy couldn't help but wonder what else would be new and special.

He also knew, to the very depths of his being, that he would never push Sam for anything, not a second kiss, not making out, not sex. Whatever was building between them was too precious to ruin by pushing for more than Sam was comfortable with. He'd just have to be patient. He wasn't a teenager anymore. He could wait.

JEREMY shifted nervously from one foot to the other as they waited for Neil or Molly to answer the door. Sam would have walked in without knocking, but Jeremy didn't feel comfortable doing that. Maybe someday he would, but not this time. Not when this was the first time he'd been invited. It was the same reason he'd insisted on leaving Arrow and Hawk in the bunkhouse despite Sam's assurances that they could come with him. Another time, maybe, but not the first time, even if Arrow got along with Max, Neil's dog, almost as well as he got along with Hawk.

"Sam, Jeremy, come in," Molly said when she answered the door. "You didn't need to knock."

"That's what I told him," Sam said, leaning forward to kiss his soon-to-be sister-in-law on the cheek. "He insisted it wouldn't be polite the first time he came over."

"I'll accept that this time," Molly said with a smile as she opened the door wider to let them in. "Neil, Sam and Jeremy are here!"

Jeremy heard a muffled voice from the other room but no words he could distinguish. Remembering his mother's lessons, he tugged off his boots and left them at the door with the collection of other shoes and boots that were there. Then he followed Sam and Molly deeper into the house. It was smaller than the big house, but from what Sam could tell, it had been built in very much the same plan as the house where Macklin and Caine now lived: living room and kitchen downstairs and a stairwell leading up to the bedrooms. Then again, from the little Jeremy could tell, most of the houses on the station with more than one bedroom followed that plan, so it should have come as no surprise that the foreman's house was the same.

"I have Carlton Old and Toohey's," Neil said, coming into the living room. "Molly insisted we get wine for dinner, but I thought you'd prefer a beer beforehand."

Jeremy hid a smile at Neil's put-upon expression. "I'll have a Carlton. Thanks."

"You could say hello, Neil," Molly chided.

"I did," Neil protested. "I offered him a beer and everything!"

"You offered him a beer. You didn't say hello," Molly corrected.

Neil rolled his eyes and turned back to Sam and Jeremy. "Hello, Jeremy," he said.

Jeremy couldn't help the snicker that escaped. "Hi, Neil. Thanks for the invitation."

"Any friend of my brother's, and all that," Neil said with a wave of his hand. "Let me get that beer. Sam, you want a Toohey's, right?"

"Yes, please."

"Come in and have a seat," Molly said. "Are you settled in all right? Is the bunkhouse comfortable?"

"It's fine," Jeremy said. "Nothing fancy, of course, but it's warm and dry, and really, what else can you ask for?"

"I could think of a few things," Molly said with a laugh, "but then I'm a decorator. I want everything to have a personal touch."

"Yeah, the bunkhouse isn't terribly personal," Jeremy said, "but it's better than my other alternatives this time of year."

"Did your brother really kick you off Taylor Peak?" she asked. "I'm sorry, that's really not my business."

"It's fine," Jeremy said. "And yes, to answer your question, he told me not to come back until I was ready to toe the line and get married. He might've said a few uncomplimentary things about Caine and Macklin while he was at it. I've never agreed with him about that, but I might have ignored it. I couldn't ignore the rest."

"No, of course not," Molly said. "You did the right thing coming here. Neil, you should talk to Macklin about getting started on a house for them."

Jeremy coughed in surprise. "The bunkhouse is fine," he said. "Really."

"It's fine now," Molly said. "But how are you going to feel in August, when the bunkhouse is full and everyone is looking at you oddly if you want to spend some time together?"

"We'll just come over here," Sam said.

"You're always welcome here," Neil said, "both of you, but our living room isn't all that much more private than the bunkhouse. If you're really going to do this whole couple thing once Sam's divorce is final, you need somewhere of your own. Unless you're thinking of going to another station."

"Not unless Macklin fires me," Jeremy replied. "I don't have to worry about getting beaten up or looked down on or poked fun at here. I'd end up always looking over my shoulder anywhere else. That doesn't mean we need to bother Caine and Macklin about a house, though. I don't want to put a strain on the station's resources."

"Just remember that it's easier to build in the winter than in the summer because there's less going on," Neil said. "If we don't do it now, you could be looking at a full summer in the bunkhouse before we'd really have time to work on it."

"I'll think about it," Jeremy said.

SAM shivered as he climbed in bed. June had turned unexpectedly cold, and today was the worst by far. Even with his long underwear on, he hadn't felt warm all day. He could only imagine how bad it had been for the jackaroos out in the paddocks. He pulled the blankets up and tried to think warm thoughts, but the wind whistled under the eaves of the bunkhouse, and Sam swore he could feel every gust through the walls and his blankets. Hawk had curled up next to him, but while her body was warm, she wasn't big enough to do more than keep a few fingers from freezing. Rationally he knew that was ridiculous. The bunkhouse was weatherproof and heated, but Sam still couldn't get warm. He thought wistfully about Neil's suggestion that he and Jeremy build a house of their own on the station, a house where they could turn up the heat as high as they wanted or snuggle together under the blankets without worrying about what anyone else thought. It was a nice idea, but it wouldn't help him tonight.

"This is stupid," he muttered. "There are dozens of other rooms. I'll just get a blanket from one of them." He pulled his jeans and shirt back on so he wasn't running around in his underwear, even the long kind, in case Jeremy was still up, and went into the room next to his. He rummaged through the low chest, looking for a blanket. He pulled one free and shook it out. A plastic bag fell from the folds and landed on his foot. With a frown, he picked it up, trying to figure out what it contained. It took a minute for the particular shape of the leaves to register. "Oh, shit. Jeremy!"

"What's wrong?" he heard Jeremy call from the other room.

Holding the bag like it might bite him, Sam headed toward the common area. "I, um… I found this when I went looking for another blanket. I don't think it's supposed to be here."

Jeremy took the bag from Sam's hand. "No, it's not, but I'm not surprised. The first night I was here, I thought I smelled marijuana smoke mixed in with the tobacco smoke, but then I didn't smell it again after that, so I figured I'd imagined it. Obviously not."

"What do we do?" Sam asked.

"We tell Macklin in the morning," Jeremy said. "If it's just the one bag, then we get rid of it. If it's more than that, I don't know what to say, but Macklin will know."

"Should we go check now?" Sam asked.

"No," Jeremy said. "You should go to bed. Your lips are blue. We'll talk to Macklin in the morning and search the bunkhouse with his and Caine's help."

"This is going to upset them," Sam said.

"Hey," Jeremy said, grabbing Sam's arms and giving him a little shake, "unless that's your pot in your hand, you aren't the one responsible for this. That's on whoever brought that shit onto

Caine's property. You're helping by reporting it. They'll figure out whose room it was in, and they'll make sure not to hire the bloke next spring. We'll keep an eye out when we're riding to make sure the bastard didn't have a few plants hidden on the property, and we'll take care of it if he did. If you hadn't found it, the jackaroo could have come back and made a real mess of things."

"I just hate being the bearer of bad news," Sam said.

"That's understandable," Jeremy said, pulling Sam a little closer. Sam let himself be held, Jeremy's warmth a balm for body and soul. "Nobody likes upsetting people they care about, but it could be far worse if you don't tell them."

Sam considered that for a minute. He'd read stories in the paper and heard things on the news about people going to jail for growing and selling marijuana, and if the authorities found plants growing on Lang Downs, it would be hard for Caine and Macklin to prove they hadn't planted them and didn't know about them. Better to deal with it before it got to that stage. "Yeah, you're right. We'll talk to them in the morning."

"Just leave it on the table for now," Jeremy said. "There's no one else here. It'll be fine sitting there."

Sam nodded, but he didn't pull away. It felt too good to be held in Jeremy's arms. To Sam's relief, Jeremy didn't pull away either.

"You going to bed?" Jeremy asked with a grin.

"It's cold," Sam said. "I can't seem to get warm, even with Hawk curled up next to me."

"Is that why you went looking for another blanket?" Jeremy asked.

Sam nodded. "But somehow I don't think that's really going to help either when I don't feel like I have any warmth for the blanket to keep inside."

"Are you sick?" Jeremy asked.

"No, just cold," Sam insisted. "I've been like this all day. Kami's stew helped at dinner, but then I went back outside to come here, and that undid all the progress I'd made."

"If it were September, I'd have a few suggestions for you," Jeremy said, waggling his eyebrows at Sam.

"If it were September, I wouldn't be cold," Sam retorted. "Not like this anyway. This is June weather, not September weather."

"You never know," Jeremy said. "The weather's unpredictable up here. It wouldn't be typical September weather, but I can remember a few years when we had unseasonably cold temperatures all the way into October."

Sam shivered again. "So any suggestions for mid-June instead of September?" he asked.

"Who has the bigger bunk?" Jeremy asked. "You or me?"

"I don't know. Why?"

"Because we can lie down together until you warm up," Jeremy suggested. "Once you're warm, the blankets will keep you that way, and I can go to the other room to sleep."

"That's not exactly fair to you," Sam said.

"I'm not sure either of the bunks is big enough for two full-grown men," Jeremy said. "They're only designed for one."

"I know," Sam said, "but I kind of like the idea of sleeping with you. Next to you, I mean!"

He flushed bright red.

Jeremy brushed his nose against Sam's. "I like both ideas personally, but I'm only human, Sam. I'm trying bloody hard not to jump you half the time, and sleeping next to you, waking up next to you, would make that even harder. I'm not saying I won't do it if that's what you want. I'm just saying think about what you're asking for and what it could mean."

Sam *had* thought about it. He'd thought about it a *lot*! The one kiss they'd shared on the veranda and all the evenings they'd spent in front of the fireplace drinking beer and chatting about everything from how the day had gone to their favorite memories of childhood winters had left Sam in no doubt of what he wanted and who he wanted it with. "Two and a half more months," he said. "Alison filed the papers on June 1. The court hearing is scheduled for end of July. Thirty-one days after that, I'm a free man."

"And when you are, we'll decide what we want to do," Jeremy said. "Tonight, though, we need to warm you up, so it's either me for a few minutes or a heating pad."

"I want it to be you," Sam said, trembling a little at the thought of walking down the hall and into one of the rooms with Jeremy's hand in his, stripping off the outer layers and then crawling beneath the covers like lovers, like partners. "But I think it would be safer if I went with the heating pad."

"I have one in my room," Jeremy said. "I'll get it for you."

Sam nodded, but he didn't move his arms from around Jeremy's waist. Jeremy chuckled and tapped Sam's wrists. "You have to let me go if I'm going to get it for you."

"In a minute," Sam said. He couldn't pin down why he was so clingy tonight, other than the cold, but he wasn't going to deny himself when it felt so good and wasn't hurting anyone.

"Okay," Jeremy said, settling his arms back around Sam's waist. "Just let me know when you're ready."

Sam leaned against Jeremy and took a deep breath. Jeremy must have taken a shower before dinner because he smelled of cedar and mint, not of dust and animal. He slid one hand over Jeremy's nape, playing idly with the short hair there. "Sam, sweetheart," Jeremy said, his breath tickling Sam's ear, "unless you're changing your mind about where you're sleeping tonight, you need to stop teasing me. I'm not made of stone."

Sam inhaled sharply and pulled back. "I'm sorry. I didn't mean to—"

Jeremy silenced him with a kiss.

"Don't ever apologize for wanting to touch me," Jeremy said when he lifted his head. "I would love nothing more than to take you back to my bunk and keep you warm all night long. I just need you to be aware of what it does to me when you touch me, and to keep that in mind when you do, okay?"

"Okay," Sam said shakily. "I know this isn't fair to you."

"Hey, I knew what I was getting into when I signed up for this gig, remember? You told me up front that your divorce wouldn't be final until September. Just because it's harder than I thought it would be doesn't mean I regret my choice. Once it's legal, though, we're going to run away for the weekend someplace where no one knows us, and we're going to spend the entire weekend in bed."

Sam shivered from desire this time instead of cold. "That sounds amazing. If you keep talking like that, I might not need that heating pad."

"If I keep talking like that, I'm going to forget it isn't September yet," Jeremy replied. This time when he pulled back, Sam let him go.

Jeremy disappeared down the hall and came back a minute later with an electric heating pad. "Plug that in and stick it between the blankets and it should warm you up nicely," Jeremy said, handing it to Sam.

"Thanks," Sam said. He set the bag of marijuana on the table and headed back toward his room, heating pad in hand. When he reached the door, he turned back to look at Jeremy. "September can't get here fast enough,"

Jeremy tensed, as if fighting himself. Sam took that as his signal to hide. He stepped into his room and closed the door.

Between the heating pad, Hawk, and the extra blanket, he was finally able to shake the chill, but his dreams that night were filled with shadowy images of a hard body wrapping around his from behind, holding him close, keeping him warm.

SIXTEEN

"Do you have a minute, Macklin?" Sam said after breakfast the next morning.

"Of course," Macklin said. "Is there a problem?"

"Kind of," Sam said. "I was going to talk to Caine, but I haven't seen him this morning."

"He went in to Boorowa with Patrick," Macklin said. "He should be back tonight. Do we need to wait for him?"

"No, I guess not," Sam said. "Could you come to the bunkhouse?"

Macklin nodded, and Sam led the way down the main road to the bunkhouse.

"I was cold last night," Sam began by way of explanation, "so I went into one of the other rooms to get a blanket. I figured I could always wash it and put it back before we hired new people in the spring, so it didn't seem like it would be a problem."

"It's not as far as I'm concerned," Macklin said. "If you need to keep it, we can always buy an extra blanket."

"No, I'm sure I won't need it later, but that's not the problem," Sam said as they walked inside. He picked up the baggie and handed it to Macklin. "I found that wrapped up in the blanket."

Macklin's face tightened. "Which room?"

Sam showed him.

"Jenkins," Macklin spat. "I should have known. He spent the entire summer doing as little work as possible. Is this all there was?"

"I don't know," Sam said. "I called Jeremy, and he said we should wait and show you this morning and search then."

"Okay," Macklin said, going into the room Jenkins had used. "Let's start searching."

They spent the next twenty minutes going through the entire room, opening drawers, checking the bottoms as well as the insides, going through the closet and the linens, even flipping the mattress to make sure it hadn't been cut open and repaired, but they didn't find any other signs of marijuana or other drugs in the room.

"We need to check the other rooms too," Macklin said when they were done. "We need to make sure he didn't hide it anywhere else or that no one else had any."

"There's nothing in the office that needs my attention today," Sam said. "I can search in here if you need to do other things."

Macklin considered that for a moment. "If you're sure you don't mind, the other concern this raises is where he got it. There was a grazier up in Cowra with a similar problem a few years ago. They found plants on his land, and he nearly went to jail over it before one of his jackaroos admitted to planting them himself. I'll feel a lot better after I've had a chance to make sure the same thing hasn't happened here."

"Do what you need to do," Sam said. "I'll search in here, and if I find anything else, I'll make a note of where it was. Don't ride out by yourself. Make sure you take someone with you."

Macklin smiled, even if it was a little tight around the edges. "I'll get Jeremy to go with me since he already knows what's going on. Don't say anything about this to anyone but Caine until I say so."

"I won't," Sam promised.

"JEREMY, saddle up!" Macklin ordered, walking into the shed where Jeremy and several of the other jackaroos were working on equipment maintenance.

"What's up, boss?" Jeremy asked as he rose from his place.

Macklin didn't reply, but the tilt of his head toward the paddock where the horses were kept was answer enough for Jeremy. Macklin might not want to talk about it in front of the others, but Jeremy could guess. He grabbed a saddle and bridle from the tack room and followed Macklin outside, with Arrow on his heels.

A few minutes later, they were headed toward the far end of the valley. "You don't think he would have planted down this way?" Jeremy asked.

"Too dangerous," Macklin said. "In the valley itself, he ran the risk of someone seeing it. If he was growing it, he had to have the plants out in one of the upper paddocks, probably away from the roads and the direct routes between drover's huts."

"So are we just riding at random or do you have an idea where it might be?" Jeremy asked.

"Jenkins usually volunteered for the team that was riding toward the south paddocks," Macklin said. "Maybe that's coincidence, and I didn't have any reason to suspect anything at the time, but it seems worth checking out."

Jeremy nodded and followed Macklin through the gate.

TWO hours later, with a storm brewing on the horizon and the temperature falling, Jeremy was reconsidering the wisdom of their search. "We need to head back," he said. "We can search more tomorrow if you're not satisfied we've checked everything out."

Macklin looked like he wanted to argue, but he scanned the horizon and relented. "I'll talk to Caine tonight when he gets back." He looked at the horizon again. "Or tomorrow, if this gets bad enough to keep him in Boorowa. I know none of the year-rounders are involved. We can trust them to help us keep an eye out. I just want to tell Caine first."

Jeremy nodded and turned his horse back the way they'd come. He'd urged it to a canter when a sharp crack of thunder startled him. For a moment, he thought he was going to lose his seat as the horse reared up in surprise, but he finally got him under control. He turned back to check on Macklin, only to see the foreman on the ground, his horse standing over him.

"Shit," Jeremy said, guiding his horse back toward Macklin. "Are you all right?"

"I don't think so," Macklin said. "I'm pretty sure I felt something in my knee go when I fell."

Jeremy frowned and slid down off his horse. He knelt next to Macklin and probed his leg gently. Macklin hissed in pain. "Yeah, something is definitely not right."

"Where's the radio?" Jeremy asked.

Macklin handed it to him. Jeremy clicked it on and called back to the station. Nobody answered. He switched the station and tried again.

"Nothing," he said.

"It could be the storm interfering with the reception, or it could be the batteries. I left it on the charger last night, but maybe it didn't take."

"So what do we do now?" Jeremy asked. "If I help, do you think you can ride?"

"Not far," Macklin said. "There's a drover's hut over the next rise. If I can get there, you can go back for a ute. Even if the storm breaks, I'll be okay until you can come back for me."

"I don't like the idea of leaving you alone."

"I'm not going to make it back to the valley on a horse," Macklin said. "At least not on Ned. Maybe if you'd ridden Titan, we could switch, but there's no way I can stay on Ned or Cloudy with a busted knee."

Jeremy pursed his lips. "Okay, let's see if we can get you on Cloudy. I can walk Ned to the drover's hut and leave him in the shed there."

They managed to get Macklin on Cloudy's back with quite a bit of swearing, but it was enough to prove Macklin's point to Jeremy. However unhappy Jeremy was at the idea of leaving

Macklin alone in the drover's hut, Macklin wouldn't make it back to the station like this, even if Jeremy could ride Ned. They made it to the drover's hut and undertook the painstaking process of getting Macklin off the horse without hurting him even worse. Jeremy dropped Cloudy's reins to steady Macklin and the horse took advantage, galloping away the minute he could. Arrow bolted after him, barking madly, but the kelpie was no match for a horse. Jeremy whistled for him to come back. It was going to be a long, miserable walk back to the station.

"Ride Ned," Macklin said as Jeremy helped him hobble inside.

"I thought you said nobody else could ride him," Jeremy said.

"What other choice is there?" Macklin asked. "The radio isn't getting through. If you walk, even if the storm doesn't break, it'll be hours before you get back. Ride Ned."

"If he throws me off and I break my neck, I'm blaming you," Jeremy threatened.

"Just… just talk to him before you mount," Macklin said. "Tell him who you are and what you need him to do. I know it makes me sound like a right Galah, but that's what I do. Every time I ride him, I remind him it's just me and tell him what we're going to do that day. The drongos who try to ride him to prove themselves never bother."

"Okay," Jeremy said. "If that's what I need to do, I'll try it. Do you need anything before I leave?"

Macklin shook his head. "I can get a fire lit and wrap up in a blanket. You won't be gone long enough for me to need more than that."

Jeremy hoped Macklin was right. "Fine, but I'll get the fire started. You can feed it from a chair, but getting down to start it would be bad for your knee."

Macklin scowled, but Jeremy ignored him. He laid a fire quickly in the grate and got it going. Meanwhile, Macklin got a blanket off one of the cots and positioned himself in a chair near the hearth. Jeremy grabbed a bottle of water and put it within Macklin's reach as well. "You have the radio, right?"

"Yes," Macklin said.

"Keep trying to get through. Just in case Ned doesn't cooperate and I end up having to walk back," Jeremy said.

"I will," Macklin said, "but he'll cooperate."

"Arrow, stay with Macklin," Jeremy told the kelpie. It would be a fast, hard ride back to the station, assuming Ned would let him ride, and Jeremy didn't want to do that to his dog.

Jeremy wished he could be so sure, but he pushed down his nerves as he went back out to where Ned waited patiently. He stroked the big horse's nose, relieved when he didn't try to take a bite out of Jeremy's hand. "Hi there, Ned," he said. "I'm Jeremy. I'm a friend of Macklin's. He's in the drover's hut, and he's hurt. He needs us to get help for him, which means I need you to let me ride you, okay? We're going back to the station. We're going to find Neil or Ian or any of the others, and we're going to bring a ute back here for Macklin so we can get him back to the house and get him patched up. Will you help me do that?"

Jeremy felt a little ridiculous talking to a horse that way, but Ned butted Jeremy's sternum with his nose, and Jeremy figured that was as good a sign as he was likely to get. He flipped the reins over Ned's head and moved to stand by his side. "I'm just going to climb up in the saddle now, okay? I'm not doing anything you need to worry about. Just like Macklin does, right?"

Ned shifted a little, but he didn't fight as Jeremy swung up into the stock saddle and got the stirrups adjusted to the right length. Macklin was a couple of inches taller, with much longer legs. "Okay, you ready to take me back to the station?" Jeremy asked Ned.

Ned shook his head, the movement carrying all the way down his arched neck to his withers. Jeremy leaned forward a bit and patted the quivering shoulder with a gloved hand. "Relax, mate," he said. "I know I'm not Macklin, but I'm not going to hurt you. All I need is for you to take me back to the station so I can bring help back to your buddy. Let's go, okay?" He moved the reins to guide Ned back toward the station.

Ned took the cue this time, starting toward the station at a brisk canter. Jeremy relaxed into the motion with the ease of an experienced rider. He might not know this horse, but he'd been riding since he could walk, and Ned's gait was smooth and easy. He could see why Macklin enjoyed riding him.

Ned shied a little when a flash of lightning lit up the darkening sky, but he settled again after a minute. Jeremy breathed a sigh of relief. He didn't want to take a tumble off Ned and lose his fastest means of transportation back to the station.

On the ride out, he and Macklin had taken their time, searching for marijuana plants as they went, but Jeremy had no time for leisurely riding now, and Ned sensed his urgency, keeping to a ground-eating lope, the kind of speed he could maintain for some time without growing winded. On Taylor Peak, with horses he knew better than Ned, Jeremy might have pushed a little harder, sure of the horse's stamina, but while he didn't doubt Ned's abilities, this was Macklin's horse, and Jeremy wouldn't take unnecessary chances with him.

"Where's Macklin?" Neil shouted as soon as Jeremy got close enough for him to see Jeremy on Ned.

"He's hurt," Jeremy said, vaulting off Ned's back and tossing the reins to the nearest jackaroo. He didn't even bother to see who it was. If Ned bolted, it would only be toward the paddock and the relative comfort it provided. "Cloudy made a run for it. I got Macklin to a hut and came back on Ned."

"You're either really brave or really stupid," Neil said. "Which hut?"

"I'll take you," Jeremy said, "but someone needs to call the doc. Macklin's knee's busted. I don't think it's broken, but somebody needs to look at it. By the time we get there and back, the doc will be here."

"Ian, call Doc Peters. Tell him Macklin has a busted knee. Jeremy and I will get him back here. And call Caine. I don't know what he was doing today, but he'll want to know as soon as possible, even if he can't get here before the doc does."

"Got it," Ian called back, heading into the house. He appeared a moment later and tossed Neil a set of keys.

"Let's go," Neil said. Jeremy climbed into the other side of the ute and told Neil which road to take out of the valley.

"What were you doing out, anyway?" Neil asked. "The weather forecast said to expect storms. Macklin told everyone to stay close to home."

"Sam found weed in the bunkhouse last night," Jeremy said. "Macklin wanted to make sure there wasn't any growing on the station."

"Drongo," Neil muttered. "He didn't think it could wait for a day?"

"Apparently not," Jeremy said. "He and Sam tore the bunkhouse apart looking for more. Fortunately they didn't find any."

"Did you see anything when you were out?"

"No," Jeremy said, "but we didn't cover the whole area Macklin wanted to check before the clouds got threatening enough for us to decide to head back."

As if on cue, the skies opened, pouring down rain.

"Bloody weather," Neil cursed. "I don't know if Doc Peters will be able to fly in this. If he has to drive from Cowra, he might not get here today."

"We can ice Macklin's knee, and I can bind it up," Jeremy said. "Doc Peters will still need to check it out, but we can get him through the night. It was just his knee, as far as I could tell."

The ute lurched and slid on the muddy road, but Neil drove like one familiar with the terrain, often moving onto the grass to get better traction.

Jeremy pulled the hood of his Driza-Bone up each time they got to a gate and dashed through the rain to open it for Neil to drive through, and the fact that Neil stopped each time as soon as the bumper was clear of the fence made Jeremy smile. They might not be friends yet, but Neil was making an effort for Sam's sake, and Jeremy appreciated it.

"How well did you know Sam's ex?" Jeremy asked when he was back in the ute again, holding his hands in front of the heater.

"I would have said fairly well until he got here," Neil said. "Now I'm not sure. Why?"

"He's convinced she'll use our relationship against him if she finds out," Jeremy said. "I was just curious if he was right or just being careful."

"Do you blame him?"

"Not at all," Jeremy said quickly. "After everything he's said, I wouldn't put anything past her. I just wanted your opinion."

"Getting tired of waiting?"

"Tired in the sense of wishing it was September already," Jeremy said. "Not tired in the sense of giving up on him, if that's what you're worried about."

"That thought never crossed my mind," Neil said. Jeremy couldn't tell if it was the truth of a convenient white lie, but he accepted it at face value.

"I want him free of her," Jeremy said, "not the least because I hate feeling like I can't even kiss him without looking over our shoulders or without feeling guilty about it. Before you ask, that's all we've done, and only a few times, and it's all we will do until he's a free man. I won't be the cause of him feeling guilty. I don't want our relationship tainted by that."

"I wasn't going to ask," Neil said. "I appreciate your honesty, but really, I don't need details of my brother's sex life. I didn't want them when he was married and it was something that made sense to me. I certainly don't need them now."

"Still a little weirded out by the whole gay business?" Jeremy asked.

"Yeah," Neil said. "I'm not angry. I'm not going to turn on him or say anything to him, but that doesn't mean I want to *think* about it. It also doesn't mean I'll let you hurt him the way Alison did. If you do, I'm coming after you."

"I don't know what will happen in the future," Jeremy said slowly, "but I promise I will never treat him the way Alison did, even if somehow things don't work out and we end up going our separate ways."

"That's fine," Neil said. "The problem isn't that they broke up. The problem is what the relationship did to him."

SEVENTEEN

CAINE'S phone chimed as he neared the outskirts of Canberra. Someone must have called while he was in the dead zone between Boorowa and Canberra. It chimed again a minute later. Frowning, he picked up the phone and looked more closely.

Not one message. Four messages. That wasn't good.

He found a parking lot and pulled into it so he could listen to the messages.

"Caine, it's Ian. Jeremy just came back riding Ned. He said Macklin's been hurt. We've called for a doctor, but I thought you'd want to know as soon as possible."

Caine felt his heart squeeze tight in his chest. The thought of something happening to Macklin tore at him. Macklin hadn't even planned on riding out today. Caine had asked. And now something had dragged him out into the tablelands, and he'd gotten hurt.

"Caine, it's Ian again. I just realized how my last message sounded. Jeremy said he hurt his knee. Badly enough he couldn't ride back in, but not life-threatening or anything. Call when you get the message."

Then, "Caine, it's Kyle. Doc Peters is flying in to look at Macklin's knee. Jeremy and Neil went to bring him back in. It's pretty badly swollen, but it doesn't seem like anything's broken."

And finally, "Caine, where are you?" The sound of Macklin's annoyed voice relieved most of Caine's worries. If Macklin was annoyed, he couldn't be in too much pain. "Call me when you get this message. I need you to pick some things up in Boorowa before you head back."

Taking a deep breath to calm himself, Caine dialed the number for the station and waited for someone to pick up.

"Where are you?" Macklin demanded. "You didn't answer your phone."

"I just now got your message," Caine said, avoiding the question. He had come too far to ruin the surprise now. "You said you needed me to pick some things up in Boorowa. If you'll give me the list, I'll make sure to get them before I head home."

Macklin gave him a list of medicines from the doctor that Caine wrote down dutifully. He hadn't planned on stopping again in Boorowa after he picked up Macklin's mother, but the prescription would be at the pharmacy there, not in Canberra, so he'd have to make an extra stop.

"Are you sure you're not hurt worse than you're telling me?" Caine asked when Macklin didn't seem in any hurry to end their conversation.

"Doc Peters checked me out pretty thoroughly," Macklin replied. "He said it's just my knee. I just hate being cooped up and helpless. If you were here, we could sit in the office together and work on the books or the organic certification application or something, so I wouldn't be stuck here on the couch by myself with nothing to do."

"Read a book," Caine suggested. "Watch TV. Work on the organic certification application yourself. I'll go over it with you when I get home if you want."

Macklin grunted.

"I'll be home as soon as I can," Caine promised. "And you said you weren't riding out today before I left, so don't blame me for not being there when you changed your plans."

"Something came up," Macklin said. "We'll talk about it when you get home."

That didn't sound good, but Caine didn't push. If Macklin didn't want to talk about it over the phone, pushing for details would only annoy him, and that was the last thing Caine wanted at the moment. He set it at a fifty-fifty chance of Macklin being annoyed with him when he got home with his surprise anyway. No reason to tip those odds against him.

"I'll be home as quickly as I can," Caine said. "I love you."

"I love you too," Macklin said. "Talk to you soon."

Nerves churning in his stomach again, Caine put down the phone and drove the rest of the way to the apartment building where he was supposed to meet Sarah Armstrong. It wasn't quite public housing, but it wasn't much better. He grinned, thinking of the house on Lang Downs and the guest room there. If this weekend went well, he'd see about moving Sarah to the station. Macklin's mother deserved better than this. He parked and went inside, looking for her apartment. He knocked on the door when he found it and waited, heart pounding, for her to answer.

He'd told her about him and Macklin, and her only reaction had been to be glad Macklin was happy, but he was still meeting his partner's mother for the first time. Without him (which probably made it easier, honestly, since they hadn't seen each other in thirty years). He didn't think she would react badly to him now, but it didn't settle his nerves completely.

The door opened, and Caine caught his first glimpse of his mother-in-law. He didn't know how old she was, but it seemed every one of her years was etched into her face. She smiled when she saw him, though, and that took a decade off her lined face. "You must be Caine."

"Yes, m-m-ma'am," he said, cursing his stutter silently, but the combination of worry about Macklin and nerves at meeting Sarah was too strong to overcome easily.

"Come in for a moment," she said. "I'm all packed. Unless you'd like a spot of tea before we go?"

"I would r-rather we g-go," Caine said. "M-Macklin got hurt today while I w-w-was d-driving here, and I'd l-like to g-get back to him as qu-quickly as possible."

"Oh, of course!" Sarah said. "I'll just get my bag."

She disappeared into the other room and came back with a small rolling suitcase. Caine took it from her and carried it out into the hall. She locked the apartment and followed him outside. "I hope it's nothing serious."

"He fell off his horse," Caine said. "He t-twisted his knee. He'll be f-fine, but I want to get home as quickly as we can."

He put the suitcase in the trunk (and smiled as he did because he still thought of it that way and not as the boot. He'd picked up a lot of the vernacular, but that wasn't one of them) and joined Sarah in the car.

"So tell me about yourself," Sarah said as Caine started back toward Boorowa. "How did you end up on a sheep station in New South Wales?"

Caine smiled. He could do this part. "My great-uncle owned Lang Downs," he explained, his stutter fading as he relaxed into the ease of storytelling. "He didn't have any children, so when he died, it passed to my mother. She was going to sell it. She didn't have any need for a sheep station, after all, but I convinced her to let me run it. Last year at Christmas, she gave it to Macklin and me."

"That was very brave of you, leaving everything to come here," Sarah said.

Caine shrugged. "There wasn't much to leave, honestly. You've heard me stutter. It's hard to get ahead in business talking that way, and I didn't have a boyfriend. The station was a godsend, a chance for a fresh start."

"It was still a brave choice," Sarah insisted. "Plenty of people stay in miserable lives because they don't have the courage to change anything."

Caine didn't ask if she was talking about herself. He didn't know what had happened to Macklin's father, but she had clearly been the only inhabitant of her apartment, so wherever he was, he wasn't bothering Sarah anymore. "It was a gamble, but it's paid off in spades."

"And Macklin?"

"Macklin is the station's foreman," Caine explained. "He helped me get my feet under me, and I fell in love with him."

"I know that wasn't as simple as you make it sound," Sarah said with a laugh.

Caine laughed too. "No, it wasn't, but like anything worth having, it was worth the work. He's a strong, stubborn, sometimes bullheaded man, but underneath that, there's a tender heart."

"I'm glad. His father did his best to beat it out of him, but it never worked when he was a child. It's good to know that hasn't changed."

MACKLIN heard the sound of the front door opening, of Caine taking off his boots and coming into the living room. He wanted to get up and go kiss his lover, but he wasn't supposed to get up without the crutches, and he hated the bloody things.

"I'm in the living room, Caine," he called.

Caine came in and joined him on the couch, kissing him firmly before running his hand down Macklin's leg. "How bad is it?"

"It's sprained, but Doc Peters doesn't think I tore anything. A few days on the couch and then a few weeks in a bloody brace and I'll be good as new. What took you so long?"

"I have a surprise for you," Caine said.

Macklin frowned. He didn't like surprises, even if he trusted Caine enough to expect it would be a good one.

"You didn't need to get me anything," Macklin said.

"I didn't," Caine said. "I got you someone instead."

That made no sense, but before Macklin could ask what Caine meant, he heard more footsteps in the hallway, and a woman he didn't recognize stepped into the room. He looked from her to Caine and then back again before recognition dawned. "Mum?"

"Hello, Macklin," she said quietly. "I hope… I hope you don't mind that I came to see you."

"How did you find me?" Macklin asked.

"I didn't," Sarah said. "Caine found me. I know you have every reason to hate me, but I wanted to see you once, to see the man you turned out to be."

"No," Macklin said, reaching for the crutches. He struggled to his feet, waving off Caine's assistance. "No, I don't hate you. My God, Mum, it's…."

Words failed him, as did his balance, so he simply held out his arms. Tears shone in Sarah's eyes as she moved into his embrace. He buried his face in her thinning hair, unbearably relieved that she smelled like roses still. All the passage of years had not changed that one thing. "I can't believe you're here."

She hugged him tightly. "I thought of you every day," she said, her voice muffled by his shirt. "I prayed you would find a place to be safe, to grow and be happy. I never imagined…" She pulled back and looked around the room. "… this."

"Did Caine tell you about the station?" Macklin asked.

"Some," Sarah said. "Sit down. He said you hurt your knee." Macklin did as she said. "Caine told me quite a bit, but I'd like to hear it from you. I've missed out on so much."

So had he.

"I'll tell you everything you want to know, but what about you?"

"There's not much to tell," Sarah said. "Your father died eight years ago. I sold everything and moved to Canberra. I help out in the kitchen of a little restaurant to supplement his death benefits. It's nothing fancy, but with just me, I didn't need anything fancy."

Macklin pulled her into another tight hug and sought Caine with his eyes. Caine smiled and nodded as he came to sit next to Macklin.

"Maybe you'd like to stay here instead?" Caine said softly, his hand coming to rest on Macklin's back as he spoke. "We have plenty of room."

"Oh, I… no, I couldn't."

"You don't have to answer yet," Caine interrupted. "It's an open-ended offer. Take the weekend, look around. Spend time with everyone. I'll take you back on Monday like we planned, but we'd very much like it if you'd think about the offer."

"Thank you," Sarah said, smiling over Macklin's shoulder at Caine. She pulled back a little and looked at Macklin. "He's a keeper."

"Believe me, Mum. I know."

"I'll leave you two to catch up," Caine said. "I need to talk to Kami for a few minutes. I'll bring dinner to you so you don't have to go to the canteen."

Caine stood, but Macklin caught his hand before he could move away. "Thank you," he said, pouring all the love he felt into the words.

"You're welcome," Caine replied, squeezing Macklin's hand.

With Caine gone, Macklin felt his confidence founder. He hadn't seen his mother in nearly thirty years. He had no idea where to even start.

"How long have you been on this station?" Sarah asked.

"Almost since I left," Macklin said. "I spent a few months on Taylor Peak, the station you crossed to get here, but that didn't work out well. I came here right after and never left."

"And now it's yours."

"It's Caine's," Macklin said firmly. "I just help him run it."

"That's not what he told me," Sarah said. "Although he said you'd say that."

Macklin chuckled. "He knows me well."

"That's not a bad thing."

"No, it's a wonderful thing. Caine's great-uncle and his partner built this place from nothing," Macklin said. "When Michael died, the station passed to Caine's mother. She signed it over to him at Christmas, and he insisted on putting my name on the deed as well."

"Then you shouldn't belittle his gift," Sarah said. "How many people work for you?"

"Twenty or so year-round," Macklin said, "and then we hire more in the summer when there's more to do. Winter is a quiet time for us."

"I am so proud of you," Sarah said, hugging him again. "I'm sorry I couldn't be here for more of it."

"You're here now," Macklin said. "Caine found you."

"Your father never would have understood, but I think Caine's wonderful. I think it's wonderful you've found a man and a place to make you happy."

"He does make me happy," Macklin said, "and he does everything he can to make everyone else just as happy. I know the offer to have you stay here must seem sudden, but I'd like it if you did. It's the right season to decide. Winter is the time to build because there's less to do for the sheep. We could have a little house for you before spring. It wouldn't be anything fancy, but it would be yours."

Sarah studied him intently for a moment. Then she threw her arms around him with a soft sob. "Oh, my son, my beautiful, sweet boy. I have missed you."

Macklin held on tight while she cried. He patted her back awkwardly, not really sure what to do with her tears.

"I should show you your room," Macklin said when the tears slowed. "You can unpack and rest a little before dinner. It's a long drive from Canberra."

Sarah shook her head. "You shouldn't be moving around on your knee. I'll sit here with you until Caine comes back. I didn't come to see the station. I came to see you."

"DO YOU need anything?" Caine asked later that night after they'd settled Sarah in her room and retired to their own bedroom. "A glass of water? Another blanket?"

"I need you to sit down and stop hovering," Macklin muttered. "I sprained my knee. I'll be fine in a few days."

"Doc Peters said at least two weeks before you could get off the crutches," Caine insisted.

Macklin grumbled some more. "Sit down and stop hovering," he repeated grumpily. "I'm not an invalid."

Caine joined him on the bed, and Macklin reached for him, then pulled him close. "Thank you. I said it earlier, but I couldn't thank you properly, not in front of Mum."

"She knows we're lovers."

"I know," Macklin said. "She knew about me even before I ran away, but there's a difference between knowing and seeing."

"And you're a private person by nature," Caine finished. "I wasn't upset that you didn't kiss me."

"Come closer. I'll kiss you now," Macklin rumbled.

Caine grinned and scooted into Macklin's arms. "I'll never say no to that."

Macklin cradled Caine's head with his hands, bringing their lips together in a tender kiss. Caine must have known how being helpless had grated all day because he made no move to fight Macklin for control of their kiss like he often did. Instead he sank into Macklin's arms and the kiss with the gentle sweetness that was so much a part of who he was.

"You amaze me," Macklin said when he could finally bear to break the kiss.

"Me?" Caine asked in surprise.

"Yes, you," Macklin said. He dropped a quick kiss to the tip of Caine's nose. "You just… make things happen. You found my mum and convinced her to give me another chance."

"It didn't take any convincing," Caine said. "She jumped at the chance to see you again."

"Maybe, but you're still the one who found her and brought her here," Macklin asserted.

"You missed her," Caine said with a self-deprecating shrug, as if he needed no other reason than that to do what Macklin had feared would be impossible after all this time. Then again, maybe he didn't need another reason. Caine had always been one to place great value on other people's happiness.

"And now I don't have to," Macklin said. He tipped them back onto the bed, intending to roll on top of Caine and thank him properly, but pain shot up from his knee the minute it touched the bed. He fell back to the side, panting.

Caine sat up immediately, hands hovering over Macklin's leg. "What can I do to help?"

"Just give me a minute," Macklin said. The pain was already subsiding. "I'm not going to be able to fuck you into the mattress like I'd planned."

"So we'll do something else," Caine said. "I can ride you—I know how much you like that—or we can lie on our sides. You know it doesn't matter to me how we make love. It's enough that you want me."

Caine's words hadn't been intended to be inflammatory. His voice could drive Macklin to complete distraction without even a touch of Caine's hands, but this wasn't Caine's sultry voice, nor was he stuttering yet, another thing Macklin found incredibly arousing. No, Caine was simply laying out options for him to consider, but the effect was equally undeniable. Taking care to keep his bad knee propped out of harm's way, Macklin pushed Caine back onto the bed again before leaning over him as best he could and taking one tawny nipple between his teeth. Caine hissed above him, the sound bringing a smile to Macklin's lips. He lifted his head and smirked at his lover. "I'll think of something," he said simply before lowering his head and returning to the most pleasant task of leaving Caine too needy to speak.

EIGHTEEN

CAINE woke alone on Monday morning, an unusual enough occurrence that he worried for a moment that something might have happened during the night. Macklin had been grumpy the night before, but Caine had chalked that up to the knowledge that Sarah would be returning to Canberra today. They had asked her repeatedly over the weekend to come and live with them, but she hadn't given them a definite answer yet. Caine expected to listen to Macklin trying to talk her into it all the way back to Canberra.

With a groan, he stretched and climbed out of bed. He pulled some clothes on and headed toward the canteen. Macklin would either be there or on the veranda, and at this hour of the morning, the canteen seemed more likely. When he reached the living room, though, he saw a light on in the office and detoured there instead. "What are you working on so early?"

Macklin looked up and smiled absently. "Plans."

Snorting softly at the singularly unhelpful answer, Caine walked into the room and peered over Macklin's shoulder. On the paper in front of him were detailed sketches, complete with penciled-in measurements. "What's this?"

"Mum's house," Macklin said. "Maybe she isn't ready to move here yet. Maybe she won't ever be, but at least the house will be ready if she wants it." He looked up at Caine with painfully vulnerable eyes. "You don't mind, do you?"

"Of course not!" Caine said. "I invited her to stay too, if you remember. We can start work on it tomorrow, at least clearing the land, while we order building materials. If she decides not to come, we can always find someone else to use it. Seth's getting to the age where he won't want to live with Chris and Jesse much longer."

"You're assuming he'll stay," Macklin said.

"If he doesn't, someone else might come along who will want it. For that matter, Sam might want it. Or Jeremy."

"Or Sam *and* Jeremy," Macklin said with a grin.

"Or that," Caine agreed. He leaned down and kissed Macklin softly. "Show her the plans. Let her help. That might give her an extra incentive to move here. It won't just be a house of her own, it'll be a house she helped design."

"That's a good idea," Macklin said. "We can talk about it on the way back to Canberra. You don't mind if I sit in the back with her while you drive, do you?"

Caine smiled and kissed Macklin again. "Of course not. You can sit in the front with me on the way back after we've dropped her off. Unless you convince her to come back with us, of course. Then you'll want to sit in the back both ways."

"I doubt she could really come back with us right away, even if we convince her," Macklin said. "She'd have to quit her job and break her lease and everything. I think the best we could hope for would be to go back and get her next weekend."

"Then we'll go back and get her," Caine said. "Or you could stay in Canberra with her. With your knee in a brace, you can't do a lot around the station anyway."

"We'll see," Macklin said. "You're assuming she'll decide to move here on the drive back today. That's a pretty big assumption."

Caine shrugged. "Just putting it out there, that's all. You know I'm not going to complain about having you here, even with a bum leg, but if it works out for you to be with her, well, you have thirty years to make up for. I can do without you for a few days."

"I love you. I can't possibly say that enough."

Caine squeezed Macklin's shoulder. "You say it plenty. Now, I'm hungry, and I imagine you are too, and we have a long drive ahead of us, so let's go see where your mother is and get something to eat."

Macklin grumbled when Caine insisted he use the crutches to get to the canteen, but Caine refused to take any chances with Macklin's recovery. He needed his foreman back at 100 percent before they hired seasonal jackaroos in August.

Caine called upstairs for Sarah, but she didn't answer, so Caine figured she was already in the canteen. Sure enough, when they reached the area where everyone gathered to eat, they found Sarah in the kitchen standing toe-to-toe with Kami. Caine had spent over a year watching everyone run in fear of the big aborigine, but Macklin's mother seemed completely unfazed by his size or his scowl.

"I'm telling you, the eggs will be fluffier if you put a bit of milk in them. Just a splash."

"I have been running this kitchen for thirty years," Kami snarled, "and no one has ever complained about my eggs."

"Then prove yours are better," Sarah challenged. "Make them my way today and see which they like better."

"If I'm right?" Kami demanded.

"Then I'll give you my grandmother's scones recipe," Sarah said. "But if I'm right, you let me cook dinner for the men the next time I come to visit."

Caine held his breath as he waited for Kami's answer. The aborigine had tolerated Chris's help when he first arrived and his broken arm kept him from working with the other jackaroos, but Chris had always been an assistant, doing whatever Kami told him and nothing more. Sarah was talking about taking over.

"I'll let you help me cook dinner," Kami amended. Caine wanted to tell Sarah to take the offer since she wouldn't get a better one, but he didn't want to break the moment.

"Deal," Sarah said, holding out her hand for Kami to shake. Kami looked at it the way Caine had seen the jackaroos eyeing a death adder when they stumbled across them in the bush. After a moment, he shook it, but the disconcerted look never left his face.

Caine tipped his head toward the dining area of the canteen. Macklin nodded, and they withdrew from the kitchen as quietly as they could. Caine had a suspicion they'd be hearing from Kami on the subject of Sarah and her "interfering ways" if she won the bet. Caine didn't even care. It would be worth it to see someone challenge Kami's absolute rule of his kitchen.

"I've never seen her stand up to someone like that," Macklin said softly when they were out of earshot.

"She lived with your father long enough to recognize the signs of someone abusive," Caine said. "Kami might grumble and even yell, but he'd never raise his hand to anyone. I'm sure she senses that. There's no danger in arguing with Kami the way there was in arguing with your father."

"I'd have his head if he did," Macklin growled.

Caine laid a gentle hand on Macklin's arm. "I'd have his job, which would undoubtedly be worse, but that isn't why he'd never do it. He just isn't that kind of man."

"I know," Macklin said with a shake of his head, as if to clear his thoughts, "but I spent fifteen years watching him hit her. It's hard to let go of the need to protect her."

"I never said that," Caine said. "You'll always want to protect her, and that's a beautiful thing. You just have to recognize what is and isn't a threat. Protect her from actual threats, not from everyone who might approach her."

Macklin groaned. "You're going to make me think about my mother dating someone, aren't you?"

"You never know," Caine said. "Uncle Michael lived into his nineties. If your mother lives as long, she might appreciate some companionship. She's only what? Seventy?"

"Sixty-five," Macklin said. "She had me when she was twenty-two."

"Then she could have thirty years of living ahead of her still. Why should she be alone all that time if she meets someone she likes?"

"She could move here. Then she wouldn't be alone," Macklin grumbled.

"She wouldn't live by herself in an empty apartment," Caine agreed, "but that's not the same as having someone to share your life with. There *is* a difference."

"Maybe, but she's my mother. I don't want to think about it."

Caine laughed. "Fine, but don't say I didn't warn you if it happens."

MACKLIN waited until everyone had gathered for dinner, even making a point of asking Jason to bring his parents to the canteen for dinner that night. When everyone had food, he hobbled to the front of the room, cursing his crutches under his breath.

"Sit down," Caine fussed, dragging a chair to where Macklin had intended to stand. "They can hear you fine."

Macklin resisted the urge to roll his eyes. His knee bloody hurt after the drive to Canberra and back, and standing on it wouldn't help, no matter how much he hated to show weakness.

"So there's good news and bad news," Macklin said after he'd sat in the chair Caine provided. "Sam found a bag of weed in the bunkhouse when he was looking for an extra blanket a few nights ago. It was in the room Jenkins used, so he won't be back when we go to town in August, but we don't know where he got his supply. He didn't go into town any more often than anyone else, and I trust all of you to have told me if he'd asked you to pick up anything illegal for him. Our concern is whether he managed to introduce pot plants onto the station so he'd have a supply immediately at hand."

"It goes without saying that we won't tolerate that here," Caine continued. "As Macklin said, we trust all of you, which is why we're telling you this. Macklin and Jeremy already started checking the south paddocks, where Jenkins regularly volunteered to work, but the station is not small, and it's not the right season either, so we're asking all of you to help us by keeping your eyes open. It's honestly fruitless to search directly." Macklin ignored the glare Caine turned his way. "The station is too large for that, but if you see something as you're going about your other duties, we need to know about it so we can eradicate it."

To Macklin's relief, everyone nodded in agreement, none of them seeming uncomfortable with the request. He hadn't expected anyone to refuse. He just hadn't wanted them to feel accused, either of using drugs themselves or of protecting the one who had. Fortunately they didn't seem to have taken the announcement that way.

"So that's obviously the bad news," Patrick said. "What's the good news?"

"The good news is that my mother, who you got to meet over the weekend, has agreed to move to the station," Macklin said. He still couldn't quite believe she'd said yes, but he had the modified plans for her house in the office, and they'd already ordered the supplies they'd need to begin work on it. "There's space in the big house for guests, of course, but that would only be comfortable for so long, so I'm hoping you'll all be willing to pitch in and help us put up a house for her."

The cheer was nearly deafening, driving home to Macklin how completely the men and women in this room had become his family. Maybe they didn't know the details of his childhood or what had led him to run away and end up on the station, but they had clearly seen the delight he'd felt in having his mother back, and they'd taken that to heart.

"So where are you going to build it?"

"How big is it going to be?"

"When is she moving?"

The flood of questions continued, too fast and overlapping for Macklin to even begin to answer them. He met Caine's eyes and laughed with the sheer joy of the moment.

"HE LOOKS happy," Sam said to Jeremy as everyone crowded around Macklin and Caine, asking questions about Macklin's mother.

"He does," Jeremy agreed. "I've known him for a long time. Not well, necessarily, but he's always had this brooding air to him, like he carried the weight of the world on his shoulders."

"He doesn't look that way now."

"No," Jeremy said, "he doesn't. I'm glad it worked out. When you first told me what Caine was doing, I was worried. I didn't know how she'd react to him and Caine or how Macklin would react to the surprise, but it looks like I worried for nothing."

"And now she's moving here," Sam said. "I'm so happy for him. I need to talk to him and Caine about something else, but it can wait until tomorrow."

"What's going on?" Jeremy asked, concerned at the subdued expression on Sam's face.

"I got the summons for the divorce hearing. I have to be in Melbourne on July 24, so I'll need at least two, possibly three days off to get down there, attend the hearing, and then get back. I don't have a car, so I'll either have to borrow Neil's or take the bus again. If I take the bus, that means someone has to drive me to Yass and come pick me up again, but I don't really feel comfortable driving off the station by myself."

"I'll come with you, if you'd like," Jeremy said, "although you'd run the risk of Alison asking who I am or what I'm doing there."

Sam was silent for so long that Jeremy grew concerned. "Sam?"

"I want to tell her to bugger off, that it's none of her business who I'm with now since she's the one who kicked me out, but I'm afraid of what she's capable of," Sam explained. "I don't want anything to delay the divorce. I've been in the closet my whole life. I can live with it for another eight weeks."

"It's up to you," Jeremy said. He certainly didn't want to do anything that might delay the divorce proceedings, but he hated the idea of Sam having to face his ex alone and without any support. "You're welcome to borrow my car, for that matter, if Neil needs his for some reason. I'm not going anywhere. Or I could drive with you as far as Seymour or one of the outlying suburbs. You could go the rest of the way in by yourself and then join me after the hearing is over. That way you wouldn't be alone."

"That's really kind of you," Sam said. "I'm not sure we should both ask Caine to be gone for three days at the same time, but I appreciate the offer."

"You don't have to decide tonight," Jeremy reminded him. "It's still over a month away. There's time to think about it and make plans."

"So how long will it take to build the house for Macklin's mum?" Sam asked.

Jeremy accepted the change of subject. "Six to eight weeks, probably," he said, "depending on how long it takes to get all the supplies. It won't be anything fancy, more like Ian or Kyle's house than like the big house. Four walls and a roof, a few interior walls, some windows... even if it isn't completely finished that fast, she'll be able to move in as they finish putting the final touches on everything."

"That's fast," Sam said. "Or maybe it isn't. I don't really have any idea how long it takes to build a house."

"It depends on how big and complicated you want it," Jeremy said, "but for something simple, it won't take that long. If you're going to stay here permanently, you might want to think about designing a place too. Living in the bunkhouse can get old after a while."

"Where else would I go?" Sam asked. "I have a job here and you're here. Unless you aren't planning on staying,...."

"The only place I'd go if I left here would be back to Taylor Peak," Jeremy said, "but it would take one hell of an apology from Devlin before I'd consider it. Until that happens, this is home."

"Then it's home for both of us. Maybe after Macklin's mum's house is done, we could talk to him about building something for ourselves."

"I'd like that," Jeremy said, squeezing Sam's hand under the table. "Since we wouldn't be paying for land, just for materials, maybe Caine and Macklin would float us a loan. It's not like we have a lot of expenses, living out here, so we could pay them back pretty quickly."

Sam smiled and returned the squeeze. "We're doing this all backward, you know. We've only kissed a few times and now we're talking about building a house together."

"You mean because we haven't slept together?" Jeremy asked. Sam nodded. "It's not about sex. It's about our relationship. I mean, I'm certainly not going to complain about being able to take you to bed when your divorce is final, but I won't love you more because of it, just like I don't love you less now for having to wait."

Sam looked completely gobsmacked. Jeremy paused for a second, trying to figure out what had put that look on Sam's face. Surely he hadn't said anything Sam would disagree with.

"Did you mean it?" Sam asked after a moment. "You really love me?"

Jeremy had to replay what he'd said for a moment before he realized what had come out of his mouth. He'd meant it. Of course he'd meant it. He just hadn't intended to say it for the first time under quite this set of circumstances.

He looked around the room at the other year-rounders. No one was paying them any attention, but he couldn't guarantee it would stay that way, and he didn't want to be interrupted. "This is the wrong place for that discussion," he said. "Let's go back to the bunkhouse, where we'll have some privacy."

Sam nodded and followed Jeremy back to the bunkhouse. Arrow and Hawk met them as soon as they stepped outside, the kitten perched, as always, on the dog's back. When they reached the bunkhouse and went inside, Sam plucked Hawk from Arrow's back and cuddled her against his chest. Jeremy felt his heart sink. That wasn't exactly the reaction he was hoping for. Sam only cuddled her like that when she asked for it or when he was upset.

Jeremy sat on the couch and patted the space next to him. Sam joined him there, Hawk still clutched tightly in his arms.

"I didn't mean to put you on the spot," Jeremy said. "It just slipped out."

"So you meant it?" Sam asked. "You love me?"

"I really meant it," Jeremy said. "I hadn't planned on bungling it quite that way or, honestly, on saying anything until your divorce went through. I didn't want you to feel pressured or like you had to stay with me just because I'd fallen for you, but—"

Jeremy never got a chance to finish his sentence because Sam kissed him. Hawk hissed between them until Sam let her go. When she squirmed her way free, Sam scooted even closer, kissing Jeremy with something approaching desperation.

Jeremy returned the kiss with the same fervor. Sam hadn't said the words back, but it didn't matter. The kiss was more than enough answer for Jeremy.

When they separated, both of them panting slightly for breath, Jeremy rested his forehead against Sam's. "So, barring the delivery, you're okay with this?"

"I think I started falling for you the first time I saw you, when you didn't back down from Neil but didn't goad him on either," Sam replied. "I just couldn't figure out—still can't figure out—what you see in me, so I didn't say anything."

There were so many things Jeremy could say to that, but he wasn't sure words would be enough to convince Sam, and yet he couldn't take him to bed and show him that way, especially not after he'd just told Sam it wasn't about the sex. Time was his greatest ally here. He'd simply keep loving Sam, keep supporting and believing in him until Sam finally woke up one day and realized how special he was to Jeremy. "I see *you*," he said. "That's all I need."

"Come with me to Melbourne," Sam said. "Alison can bugger off, for all I care. If she asks, I'll tell her you drove me in since I don't have a car, but that's as far as I'm going to let her control me now. If she wants to tell the judge I'm sleeping with you, I'll be able to honestly answer I'm not, even if the only reason I'm not is so that I can swear it before the judge, and if he decides in her favor, I'll just find a way to pay her whatever he decides I have to. I'm not leaving Lang Downs, so it's not like I have to worry about losing my job because I'm gay, or not being able to find another one, or anything like that. I've let her control me for too long."

EPILOGUE

SAM nearly turned around and walked back out of Neil and Molly's house when he saw the sign that hung in their living room: "Happy Divorce Day!"

He was certainly happy his divorce was final. He'd been waiting for this day since he and Alison had separated, even more since he arrived at Lang Downs, but to have a party? Sam was a little more private than that.

"Relax," Jeremy murmured behind him. "Neil only invited our friends, not the whole station."

Thank God for small favors.

Of course the room was still crowded. Neil's definition of their friends was larger than Sam's, not that Sam would have refused to let any of the attendees come, if asked. He just might not have invited them if he'd been given a say in the guest list.

Which was probably why Neil hadn't asked him.

"Come on," Jeremy said, urging Sam toward the table Molly had laid out full of food. "You'll be more comfortable once you've got a plate and something to drink."

Sam let himself be led. He filled the plate Jeremy gave him, seeing Kami's hand in some of the dishes as well as Molly's. Then Kami came out of Molly's kitchen with another tray, Sarah right behind him, fussing at him. Kami looked for all the world like a henpecked husband, and Sam couldn't stop the smile that spread across his face at the sight.

"Do you suppose the station will ever get used to that?" Sam asked.

Jeremy grinned. "The seasonal blokes don't think anything of it, not the new ones anyway, but no, I don't think we'll get used to it anytime soon."

Sarah had moved back to Lang Downs as expected, and the year-rounders had thrown all their effort into getting her house ready as quickly as possible. Before it was done, she had walked into the office one day while Sam, Caine, and Macklin were going over the accounts and announced that if it wasn't too much trouble, she didn't really need the house after all since she'd be moving in with Kami. Sam was pretty sure he could have knocked Macklin over with a feather right then.

Caine hadn't batted an eyelash, just turned to Sam and asked if he'd like a house, as if that had been the intention all along. Sam had agreed on two conditions: that he be allowed to pay the station back for the materials over time, and that Jeremy be allowed to move into it with him.

Caine had argued the first and looked at Sam like he'd lost his mind for even worrying about the second.

"You're blocking the line." Jeremy bumped his hip against Sam's, startling Sam out of his memories.

"Sorry. Just thinking."

"No worries." Jeremy leaned in and kissed Sam swiftly, catching Sam off guard.

"I can do that now, remember?" Jeremy said when Sam tensed automatically. "No one here cares, and no one *not* here has any say in your life anymore."

It took Sam a minute to remember. He'd gotten more confident around the year-rounders. Jeremy was right that no one at the party tonight would be surprised at seeing them kiss. They hadn't made a habit of public displays of affection, but their blooming relationship wasn't a revelation either.

Sam's sexuality hadn't come up at the divorce hearing, much to his relief. The judge had read over the settlement agreement and signed it without change or comment, and the thirty-day waiting period had passed with no contact from Alison. She was no longer a part of his life and never had to be again.

"It's not that," he said, although he still had to remind himself sometimes that it was over and he was free. "It's just… private, you know? Something for us, not for them."

"I'm certainly not planning on doing anything more than kissing you while they're around," Jeremy said, "but you don't blink when Neil kisses Molly. It shouldn't be any different when we kiss."

"It won't be," Sam promised. "I'm just still getting used to the idea that we can be together without having to hide or pretend it's less than it is. Can you be patient with me a little longer?"

"As long as you need," Jeremy replied, nudging Sam with his shoulder.

Sam smiled in relief. He'd hoped that would be Jeremy's answer. Impulsively, he leaned over and kissed Jeremy in return.

"Hey, you two," Neil shouted from across the room. "Save the making out for after the party."

Sam flipped his brother off and gave Jeremy another quick kiss.

Maybe he wouldn't need as much time as he'd thought.

ARIEL TACHNA lives outside of Houston with her husband, her daughter and son, and their cat. Before moving there, she traveled all over the world, having fallen in love with both France, where she found her husband, and India, where she dreams of retiring some day. She's bilingual with snippets of four other languages to her credit, and is as in love with languages as she is with writing.

Visit Ariel at her website http://www.arieltachna.com or e-mail her at arieltachna@gmail.com.

ARIEL TACHNA

INHERIT THE SKY

http://www.dreamspinnerpress.com

ARIEL TACHNA

CHASE THE STARS

ARIEL TACHNA

CHÂTEAU
D'ETERNITÉ

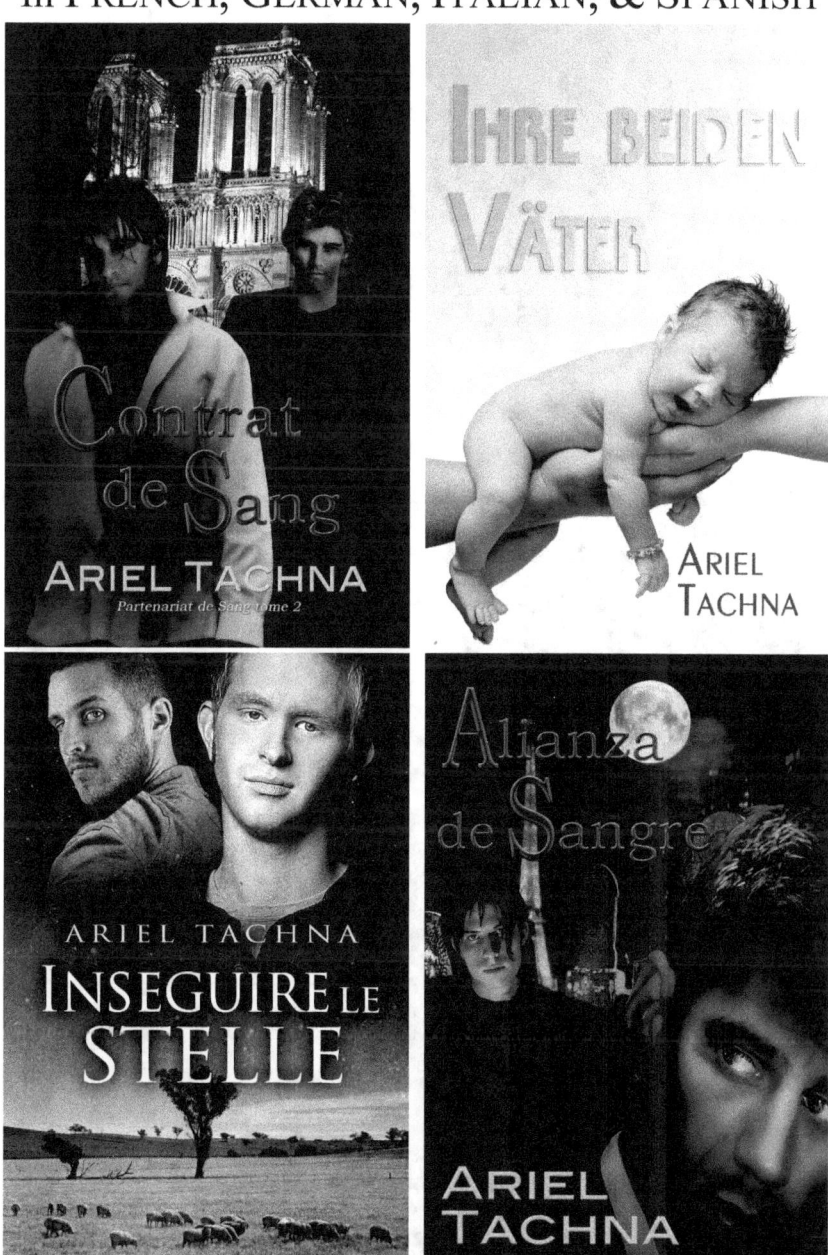

Also from ARIEL TACHNA

http://www.dreamspinnerpress.com

Also from ARIEL TACHNA

SEDUCING C.C.

Ariel
Tachna

http://www.dreamspinnerpress.com

Also from ARIEL TACHNA

http://www.dreamspinnerpress.com

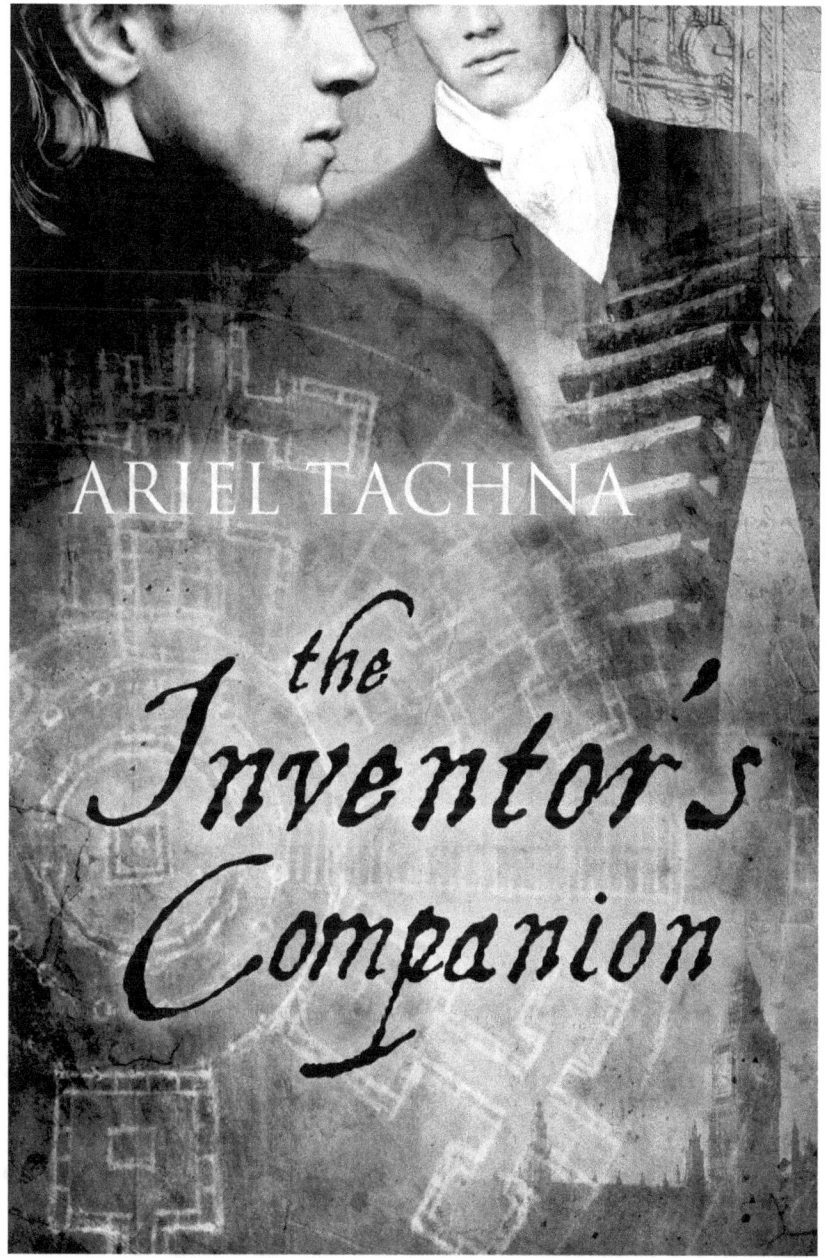

Alliance in Blood

ARIEL
TACHNA

Also from ARIEL TACHNA

ARIEL TACHNA

A Summer Place

http://www.dreamspinnerpress.com

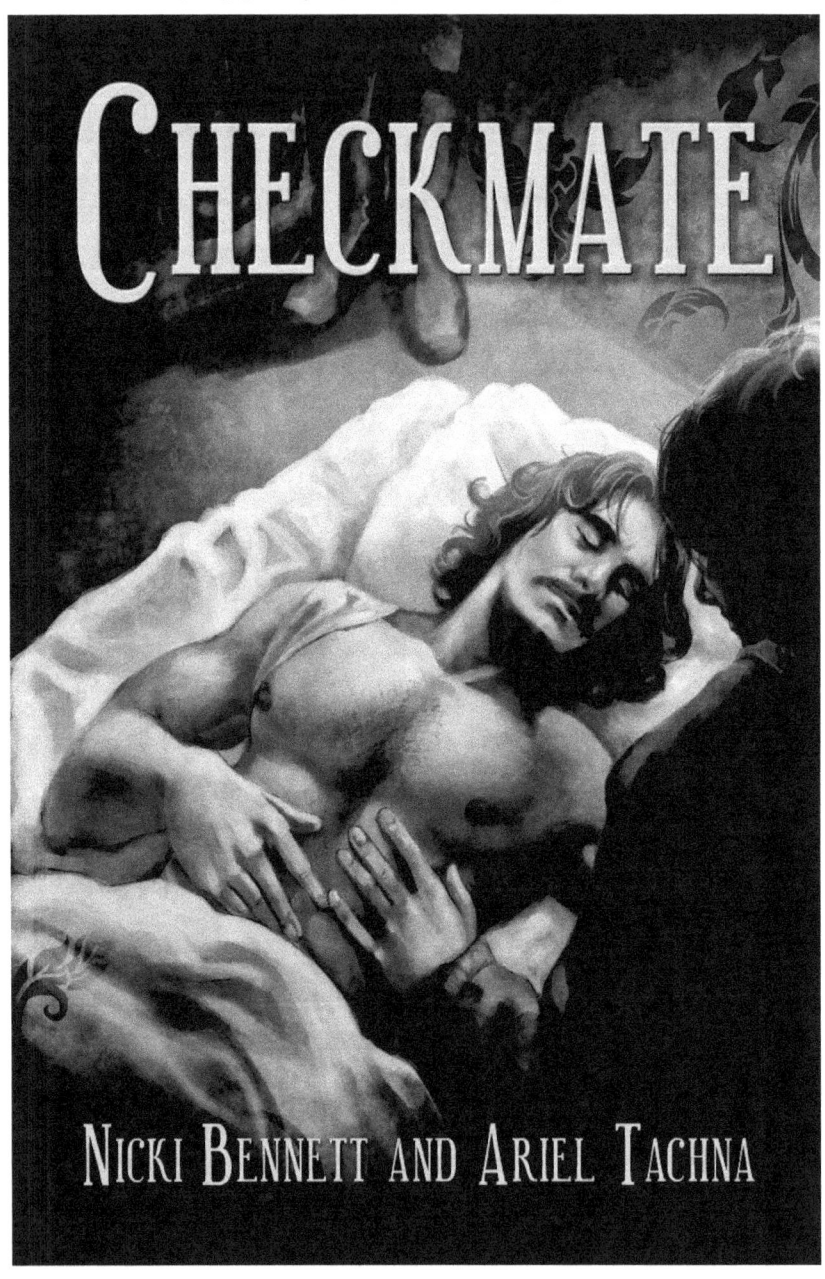

Also from ARIEL TACHNA

NICKI BENNETT AND ARIEL TACHNA

ALL FOR ONE

http://www.dreamspinnerpress.com

www.ingramcontent.com/pod-product-compliance
Lightning Source LLC
Chambersburg PA
CBHW070122260626
47160CB00004B/1583